Jobs For The Boys

Also by William Agunwa:

Treatment of Femoral Fractures. British Journal of Accident Surgery (Injury)

Osteoarthrosis of the Hips and Knees Among Rural Saudis, The British Medical Journal (Annals of the Rheumatic Diseases)

Adhesive Capsulitis of the Shoulders and Plantar Fasciitis Among Saudis Jeddah Zone, The British Medical Journal (Annals of the Rheumatic Diseases)

Jobs For The Boys

William Agunwa

Polyverse Publications
Carpinteria, CA United States

To Gudrun, Nicola and Johnathan

First published in Great Britain in 1990
Copyright © William Agunwa 1990

The right of William Agunwa to be identified as the author of this
work has been asserted by him in accordance with the Copyright,
Design and Patents Act 1988.

All rights reserved. No part of this publication may be reproduced,
transmitted, or stored in a retrieval system, in any form, or by any means,
without permission in writing from the publisher, nor be otherwise circulated
in any form of binding or cover other than that in which it is published and
without a similar condition being imposed on the subsequent purchaser.

All characters in this publication are fictitious and any resemblance to
real people, alive or dead, is purely coincidental.

Published in the USA by
Polyverse Publications,
Carpinteria, CA 93013
New Edition, 2021

ISBN 978-1-7378832-6-5

Contents

Chapter 1

My wife Rachel and I have just separated. Lately things have been very difficult, and we have been sleeping in separate rooms for the past two months or so. I am not quite sure what went wrong but our relationship seemed suddenly to have hit rock bottom soon after our only daughter, Anne, died from the severe head injury she sustained when their school bus on a trip to Whipsnade Zoo was involved in a crash in thick fog. She never really regained consciousness and was in the Intensive Care Unit of our local hospital in Hertfordshire for ninety-eight days.

Anne died on her seventh birthday when her condition suddenly became hopeless, and it was decided to switch off her life-support machines. Rachel had sat beside Anne, holding her hands, and occasionally playing her favourite pop-songs and Blue Peter recordings on a portable cassette recorder, practically every day and most nights. She never gave up hope until the day the life-support machines were switched off. Rachel and Anne were very close, perhaps because Anne saw very little of me except during my annual leave when we went on holidays together. She was a warm out-going pretty girl, with her mother's good looks.

Following Anne's accident, I took a fortnight's compassionate leave to be with my family before going back to Scotland where I had been working as a locum Senior Surgical Registrar on a long-term contract in a teaching hospital. I phoned Rachel every night from Scotland. Permanent career surgical training jobs beyond the Registrar grade were now extremely hard to come by especially if you were not a white British indigene.

Rachel had been very understanding and supportive, but she once threatened to leave me because of our unsettlingly frequent house moves (to take up the next two-years or so contract) or because her specially prepared dinner had been ruined or uneaten because I was held up doing emergency cases. Also, the dinner dates cancelled at very short notice for similar reasons.

I came down from Scotland on the Inter-City Nightrider trains every weekend I was free but arrived too late to be with Rachel the weekend when Anne's life-support machines were turned off because our train had been held up for some reason both at Edinburgh and at Peterborough. Rachel felt very upset and angry about this as if the delays were of my own making.

On my next weekend visit, whilst helping her to wash up I said to Rachel, "Listen, dear, I've got something to tell you."

"Not interested, sorry."

"You will be in this. I've got another Senior Registrarship interview coming up."

She said flatly: "Oh yes."

"But… you don't seem really interested or pleased. You used to be."

"Don't worry, I expect I will be when I get round to it."

"How do you mean?" I stared at her and seemed to read in her face an angry and obdurate resistance to me and a sufficient answer to my question. It was as if she'd taken much greater physical hurt from Anne's death than I could imagine: her eyes were narrowed, I thought, not in the familiar nervous peering, but in flinching; her neck was thinned by an apparent constriction of her throat. Her mouth tightened and she looked down at her hand, where there was a small recent burn. Then she said, falteringly a little:

"I… just don't feel like it."

"Darling…" I stepped towards her.

She looked up sharply and retreated, her eyes wide open now.

"None of that. I don't want any of that."

"I'm sorry. Can't we talk this over as we used to, sort of clear the air?"

She folded her arms and narrowed her eyes: "Just leave me in peace now."

"Rachel, I understand… Isn't there anything I can do?"

There was a stony silence.

I decided to go for a brisk walk. But as soon as I was outside the door, the wind, an old enemy of mine, sprang at me, bringing its old crony, the rain, up in support. I trod on a loose paving-stone; it tipped up and squirted cold dirty water into my shoe.

What could I do in order to hurt myself? Had Rachel really meant that our marriage was over for good? Or perhaps she'd only been angry, which of course I could… I made up my mind never again, this side of the grave at any rate, to use the word 'understand' or any of its synonyms or any item of its conjugations or derivatives, even to myself and not out loud – especially where women were concerned. If my character was, as it appeared it be, not so much insensitive or bad as unworkable, farcically unfitted for its task, like an asbestos fire-lighter, then that was more than merely bad luck for Rachel. I wished I could discover, like a galactic-federation physicist in a science-fiction story, some chink or warp in time that would age Rachel and me five years in five minutes. The alternative, presumably, was to accept myself for what I was.

Chapter 2

I took a train to the English Midlands to attend my fifth Surgical Senior Registrarship interview in the past eighteen months. I arrived a day early to discuss the post and the job description with the out-going Senior Registrar, Mr. Duncan Haynes. I was also shown around the Department.

"If you'll just wait in here, gentlemen," the Medical Staffing Officer said, "the committee will call you in one by one. Alphabetical order." He was leaving us in the waiting-room when the candidate from Southampton said:

"Excuse me just one moment."

"Yes?" the Personnel Officer said with raised eyebrows.

"Will the Committee announce their appointment today, do you suppose?"

"Naturally. Naturally they will. The result will be announced shortly after the conclusion of the last interview. And will you all please fill out the travelling expenses claim forms on that table."

"Thank you. That's exactly what I wanted to know."

We all relaxed and looked round each other as the Personnel Officer left. There were seven of us for just this single post.

The eighth failed to turn up. He had just been offered a Senior Registrarship at Oxford.

Three of the other candidates I had met at other interviews. The much-favoured local candidate who had been a Career Surgical Registrar for almost two years was the last to arrive in the waiting room. We gathered that the other Senior Surgical Registrar in the Department had been in the post for six years, and was having problems in getting a Consultant post despite having had his Accreditation two years back. One of the candidates, Malcom Anderson, was in my class in medical school. We had both shared the Clinical Surgery prize in the final year and had done our pre-registration surgical jobs in the firm of the Regius Professor of Surgery.

Malcolm was a very broad man and when we were at University was a keen Rugby player and a self-confessed extrovert. He was almost the same height standing up as sitting down. He put his great hands on his great knees and cleared his throat.

"Well, that's a relief," he said. "I shall be in first and get it over."

"Oh, you'd say that was an advantage, would you?" the Southampton man asked.

"In two ways," Malcolm said briskly. "First, they'll be fresh. Won't have had time to get sick of the job and want to get home. Secondly, first impressions stick. Nobody's been in before to set the standard."

"That's really most interesting," the Southampton doctor murmured.

"Of course, you're by the way being a bit of an expert on interviews, aren't you, Malcolm? This must be your eight one?" Adrian Bolt who knew him slightly, said.

"Ought to be Adrian, ought to be," Malcolm shook slowly with laughter.

The Southampton doctor looked from face to face, then commented: "It all seems a bit of a charade to me. Why invite so many candidates for the interview – just for the single post, and the local chap nearly always lands the job."

"It used to be said that you had to be white and British or have British connections to have any hope of getting this type of job. Now it seems your face must fit as well," whispered the candidate from Exeter to the doctor sitting next to him. "As to the numbers game, I expect the members of the Selection Committee have to earn their keep somehow. Just won't do finishing the interview in less than three to four hours," Malcom rejoined.

I tried to stop myself from despairing by reciting to myself the possible argument against each of the other candidates. As I did so, everyone seemed more and more overwhelming. For a start I was the only non-white candidate, though I was British by birth and had a British passport. I had already been to four previous interviews in the recent past for non-temporary Senior Surgical Registrarships and came away empty-handed each time, my despondency growing with each failed interview. After all, I seemed to have done the right jobs and passed my English Primary, my English and Edinburgh Finals all within twelve months, as well as spending just over a year as a Surgical Research Registrar.

Malcolm murmured to me: "How are you feeling, Desmond?"

"Not too bad," I lied.

"You're extremely fortunate to have the temperament for these things. I haven't, I must confess."

"You mustn't worry, Malcolm," I said. "You've got as good a chance as anyone else, perhaps even better this time round. I gathered that last week the local chap fell foul of his senior Consultant in theatre, and the Consultant is on the Selection Committee. Who knows how this might affect his chances?"

"I'm afraid I don't much fancy my chances, though thank you Desmond, for trying to boost my morale. It is the waiting before and especially after the conclusion of the last interview I find almost insupportable."

I was christened Desmond Smith, after my adoptive parents Alan and Mary Smith. Alan was a dental surgeon and Mary had trained as a dental nurse. They were both very active born-again evangelical Christians. Alan's parents had come originally from Edinburgh and Mary was born in Basingstoke in Hampshire. They met whilst working in the same group practice in Woking, Surrey. I was never quite sure why they didn't have any children of their own, but I later learned that Alan had had treatment for a left testicular tumour, apparently successfully, and Mary been treated for endometriosis.

Soon after I was born, of Nigerian parents who came over here to study, I was fostered out to the Smiths. I've never found out why, but in December of the same year during a cold winter snap with extreme hard frost, my natural parents' lodgings in Cricklewood, North London, where I was born, was reduced to rubble whilst they were asleep, following a gas leak explosion that ripped out a nearby street. Adjoining houses were severely damaged. My parents and one other lodger were found dead amongst the rubble.

In the waiting-room thermos flasks of tasteless instant coffee were made available for the candidates; no one seemed to care much about drinking them but there were not a few quick dashes to the lavatory nearby as the tension mounted. Adrian Bolt leaned forward to me and said: "I say, you don't happen to have a cigarette, do you?"

"I'm sorry, I don't smoke," I replied, but Malcolm Anderson was pulling out a twenty packet of low-tar Dunhill and giving it to Adrian with "Here you are, boy, help yourself."

"Thanks very much," Adrian said, opening it with all speed.

"I suppose you hadn't the chance to buy any on the train, and then when you got down here things moved a bit fast, as it were?" Malcolm asked, smiling.

"Aren't you having one yourself? Adrian said.

"No, they'll be calling me any minute now." Malcolm struck a match for him. "Won't be worth it. Don't smoke a great deal, anyway."

"Well, thank you very much." He held the packet out to Malcolm.

"No, no, keep them, Adrian. You've run out."

"But I can't let you just…"

"There are only a few in there. Go on man, put 'em away."

"But you'll be…"

"Mr. Malcolm Anderson, please," the Personnel Officer said at the threshold. "We'll, here we go, boys," Malcolm got up, gaining perhaps two or three inches in stature. "You hold on to those smokes, Adrian, now. See you all later."

Adrian wished him good luck in ringing tones. The rest of us provided a quieter echo, and he followed the Personnel Officer out. Adrian smoked away without apparent enjoyment; out of the corner of my eye I saw him sliding the cigarettes guiltily into his pocket. The Southampton doctor glanced at me, but I pretended not to notice. I wasn't so full of calm myself as to have any to lend.

I linked my hands behind my head and closed my eyes. To pass the time, I began devising the ideal interview, which would secure the ideal candidate in the minimum time.

QUESTION: What is your name?

ANSWER: Desmond Smith.

Q: And your nationality?

A: British

Q: Really?

A: I was born in London.

Q: Married?

A: Yes.

Q: Children?

A: Not now.

Q: How do you mean?

A: Our daughter died a couple of months ago in a road traffic accident.

Q: Sorry to hear that.

A: Not to worry.

Q: Why did you apply for this job?

A: I think it's as good a post as any for my Higher Surgical Training.

Q: Any special interests?

A: Rectal surgery.

Q: I see you spent two years under Professor Higginbottom at St. Marks.

A: That is correct.

Q: How did you find him?

A: An excellent teacher.

Q: Rather difficult to please?

A: Sometimes, perhaps.

Q: If appointed when will you be available to start?

A: Within two months.

Q: Any interviews in the past for Senior Registrar post in Surgery?

A: This is my fifth.

Q: Why haven't you been successful yet?

A: I don't know.

Q: Have you any questions you want to ask?

A: No, thank you.

Q: Thank you Mr. Smith. Would you mind waiting outside?

"They're a long time with Malcolm Anderson," Adrian Bolt said hoarsely.

"Oh, not ten minutes yet," I said.

The Southampton doctor glance at his wristwatch but said nothing. Some fifteen minutes afterwards the Personnel Officer re-appeared, making Adrian Bolt start with some violence.

"Mr. Bolt, come this way, please."

Adrian Bolt got to his feet, drawing in his breath. "Here we go then," he said, looking at me.

"Good luck Adrian," I said.

"All the best," the Southampton doctor croaked.

After what seemed like an eternity I was called. A numbing sense of Deja-vu overwhelmed me as I entered the Committee Room with its long, oblong, highly polished table. There was a representative from one of the Royal Colleges of Surgeons, an external assessor from Bristol and the rest of the Selection Committee including the Professor of Surgery and the Personnel Officer who had been calling the candidates.

"Sit down, please. Mr. Smith," the Professor said, smiling faintly. He was in the chair. Gradually, like a herd of big game scenting man, the member of the Committee began turning their heads in my direction. As each gaze reached my face it became keen and searching trying to sum me up. I felt more than a little hemmed in. My impression was that nobody loved me.

I was sitting at the mid-point of the longer side of the rectangular table with the Professor opposite me. There was a general introduction of the member of the Committee, and throughout the interview I was to be conscious of disquieting mutterings and fidgeting at the two lateral extremities of my vision. I wondered all the time just what the conundrum or death's head they might be rigging up for me in the flaks. I tried to show I didn't mind it much when the Committee asked each other my name, went on looking to the heart of me and turned through their sheaves of papers to find the stuff about me.

I tried to give a bodily and facial impersonation of the thoroughly good, sound, honest, reliable, trustworthy, competent, responsible, steady, sober, level-headed chap, with just that touch of imagination which makes all the difference. I moved my hips forward a couple of millimeters to indicate this last property but kept my brow trustworthy and my eyes competent.

The interview began. The Professor took me through my curriculum vitae, making sure that I wasn't an imposter, or at least wouldn't own up to being one at this stage. The rest of the interview took a pattern I had now got used to. I sensed I was not going to get the job.

I nearly left soon after my interview but curiosity to see who landed the job got the better of me. When the last man had gone in and had come out, there was a tense and anxious half hour, with some of the candidates pacing back and forth before the Personnel Officer came back to the waiting-room to say: "Would Mr. Malcolm Anderson come in again, please."

Well, that was it. At least the local chap didn't get the job this time.

Chapter 3

Rachel was born not far from the Kensington Oval in Barbados. Her father, Alistair McAlpine, a Scottish engineering consultant, was on holiday in Barbados when he met Lucy, a shapely, vivacious, and fair-skinned Barbadian who later became his wife and Rachel's mother.

It was at a party Alistair and his friend David Pringle attended at a Barbadian beach resort where they came to seek the sun a fortnight in early spring. They spotted Lucy at exactly the same moment. She was of medium height and build, and she had very shapely legs and well-turned ankles – a striking combination in both men's fantasies. Without another thought each knew exactly where he desired to end up that particular night and, two minds with but a single idea, they advanced purposefully upon her.

"Hello, my name is Alistair McAlpine."

"Hello," she replied. I'm Lucy Berrt."

"And I'm David Pringle."

She offered her hand, and both tried to grab it. When the party had come to an end, they had, between them, discovered that Lucy Berrt was a highly paid private secretary working for one of the top executives of a multinational corporation with substantial commercial interests on the island and in the Caribbean. She had majored in English, Spanish, and French at a College in New Orleans in the United States. She had then worked for a couple of years in New York and Philadelphia after finishing a course in Secretarial Studies in Connecticut, before returning home to Barbados to work for the multinational company. They had also discovered that she was a bachelor-girl with a mind of her own.

Neither Alistair McAlpine nor David Pringle was any nearer to impressing her, if only because each worked so hard to out-do the other; they both showed off abominably and even squabbled over fetching their new companion her food and drink. In the other's absence they found themselves running down their closest friend in a subtle but damning way.

"Alistair's a nice chap if it wasn't for his stinginess," said David.

"Super fellow David, such a lovely wife and you should see his two adorable children," added Alistair.

"And he's never off the bottle. He must have a stomach lined with lead to have survived all that drinking," David pursued.

They both escorted Lucy home and reluctantly left her on the doorstep of her semi-detached house. She kissed the two of them perfunctorily on the cheek, thanked them and said goodnight. They walked back to the hotel in silence. When they reached their room, it was Alistair who spoke first.

"I'm sorry," he said. "I made a bloody fool of myself."

"I was every bit as bad," said David. "We shouldn't fight over a woman like that."

They decided it was best if they went their separate way for the rest of the holiday, then climbed into their respective beds, and slept soundly.

When Alistair woke up the following morning, he was determined to get in touch with Lucy again. He couldn't get her out of his thoughts. After some painstaking enquiries he managed to get her home telephone number. Five days later Alistair called Lucy from his hotel room, wondering if she would even remember the two vainglorious men at the party almost a week before, and if she did whether she would also recall which one he was. He dialed nervously and listened to the ringing tone. Was she in, was she at another party? At last, a click and a soft voice said hello.

"Hello, Lucy, it's Alistair McAlpine."

"Hello Alistair. What a nice surprise."

"You wouldn't be free for dinner on Tuesday by any chance?"

"Let me just check my diary."

Alistair held his breath as he waited. It seemed like hours.

"Yes, that seems to be fine."

"Fantastic. Shall I pick you up around eight?"

"Yes, thank you, Alistair. I'll look forward to seeing you then."

That Tuesday evening Alistair had a long bath and a slow shave, cutting himself twice and slapping on a little too much aftershave. He rummaged around for his most telling tie, shirt, and suit, and after he had finished dressing, he studied himself in the mirror, carefully combing his freshly washed hair to make the long thin strands appear casual as well as to cover the parts where his hair was beginning to recede. After a final check, he was able to convince himself that he looked less than his thirty-five years. He then took the lift down to the ground floor and, stepping out on to the street, he headed jauntily towards Lucy's place. En route, he acquired a dozen roses from a little shop and humming to himself proceeded confidently. He arrived at the front door of Lucy's house at eight o'clock.

When Lucy opened the door, Alistair thought she looked even more beautiful than he had remembered. She was wearing a clinging long blue dress, with a frilly white silk collar and cuffs, that covered every part of her body from neck to ankles and yet she could not have been more desirable. She wore almost no make-up except a touch of lipstick that Alistair already had plans to remove. Her eyes sparkled.

"Say something," she said smiling.

"You look stunning, Lucy," was all he could think of as he handed her the roses.

"How sweet of you," she replied and invited him in.

Alistair followed her into the kitchen where she hammered the long stems and arranged the flowers in a porcelain vase. She then led him into the living room, where she placed the roses on an oval table.

"Have time for a drink?"

"Sure. I've booked a table at the restaurant of the hotel where the party was held when we first met. It's for eight-thirty."

"My favourite restaurant," she said, with a smile that revealed a small dimple on her cheek.

Without asking Lucy poured two whiskeys and handed one of them to Alistair who kept picking up and putting down his glass, like a teenager on his first date. When Alistair had eventually finished his drink, Lucy suggested they should leave.

"That restaurant wouldn't keep a table free for one minute, even if you were a millionaire pop-star."

Alistair laughed, and helped her on with her coat. She unlatched the door and once they were on the street, he hailed a taxi and directed the driver to the hotel restaurant. As they entered the crowded room Alistair could see that the place was frequented by those who were not short of a bob or two. He wondered if his pocket could stand the expense and, more importantly, whether such an outlay could turn out to be a worthwhile investment.

A waiter guided them to a small table at the back of the room, where they both had another whiskey while they studied the menu. The waiter returned to take their order. Lucy wanted no first course, just fillet steak, so Alistair ordered the same for himself.

"Looks good," said Alistair.

"Tastes good, too," said Lucy.

Alistair refilled her glass of wine nearly to the brim, hoping he could order a second bottle before she finished her steak.

"Are you trying to get me drunk, Alistair?"

"If you think it will help," he replied laughing.

Lucy didn't laugh. The waiter cleared away their empty plates.

"Can I tempt you with a dessert, Lucy?"

"No, no. I'm trying to lose some weight."

Alistair slipped a hand gently around her waist.

"You don't need to," he said. "You feel just perfect."

She felt a thrill of sexual desire course through her. She laughed. He laughed. Their eyes locked.

"Nevertheless, I'll stick to coffee, please."

"A little brandy?"

"No, thank you, just coffee."

"Black?"

"Black."

"Coffee for two, please." Alistair said to the hovering waiter.

"I wish I had taken you somewhere a little quieter," he said, turning back to Lucy.

"Why?"

Alistair took her hand. It was soft and yielding. "I would like to have said thing to you that shouldn't be listened to by people on the next table."

"I don't think anyone would overhear us."

"Very well then. Do you believe in love at first sight?"

"No, but I think it's possible to be physically attracted to a person on first meeting them."

"Well, I must confess, I was to you."

Again, she made no reply. The coffee arrived and Lucy released her hand to take a sip. Alistair followed suit.

"It's been such a lovely evening, Lucy."

"Yes, I've enjoyed it. Thank you so much," Lucy replied.

Alistair called for the bill and settled up. "Care for a stroll?"

"Why not, Alistair?"

As they strolled down the street they chatted about inconsequential affairs, while Alistair's thoughts were of only one affair. When they arrived at Lucy's place, she took out her latch key.

"Would you like a nightcap?" She asked without any suggestive intonation.

"No more drink, thank you Lucy, but I would certainly appreciate a coffee." She led him into the living room.

"The flowers have lasted well," she teased, and left him to make the coffee. She returned after a few minutes with a coffee pot and two small cups on a lacquered tray. She poured, the coffee black again, and then sat down next to Alistair on the couch, drawing one leg underneath her while turning slightly towards him.

Alistair downed his coffee in two gulps, scalding his, mouth slightly. Them putting down his cup, he leaned over and kissed her energetically on the mouth for a minute or two. She was still clutching on to her coffee cup. Her eyes opened briefly as she maneuvered the cup on to a side table and the exercise was then marked by frequent rustling changes of position and then she broke away from him.

"I ought to make an early start in the morning."

"So should I," said Alistair, "but I am more worried about not seeing you again."

"What a nice thing to say," Lucy replied.

"No, I just care," he said, before kissing her again.

This time she responded. He slipped one hand on to her breast while the other began to undo the row of little buttons down the back of her dress. He then kissed her on the neck and shoulders, slipping her dress off as he moved deftly down her body to her breast, delighted to find that she wasn't wearing a bra. She turned and put her tongue to his ear, which though noisy, was thrilling. As their physical passion swelled and throbbed and all but obliterated her, she broke away again.

"Don't let's do anything we'll regret."

"I know we won't regret it," crooned Alistair as he felt himself getting harder and harder.

Lucy squirmed away from him and started doing up her dress again.

"I'm sorry, Alistair. It's the wrong time. The mood has passed. Can't explain."

"Nothing to explain," Alistair said dryly, feeling suddenly deflated and limp.

"Can we meet again?"

"I'm sure we will," Lucy replied softly, as she unlatched the door. "Thank you again for the lovely dinner."

"Don't mention it."

Alistair took a taxi back to his hotel and wondered why it all went wrong at the last moment.

Chapter 4

"Have you got to go?" David Pringle asked his friend Alistair McAlpine who had been extremely listless, mooning away his time since they returned from their holiday in Barbados. Alistair was now determined to go back and see Lucy again. She was in his blood and the wanting of her was beginning to affect his work.

When he returned to Perth in Scotland, he had kept in touch with Lucy by phone mostly, and exactly two months after his return he was back in Barbados via the United States supposedly on a business trip. A letter was waiting for him at his hotel the morning his return when he was handing in his keys at the reception desk. It was an invitation form Lucy to meet her at the entrance of a beach hotel that evening.

Alistair arrived punctually but Lucy was almost ten minutes late. "I'm sorry Alistair," she said. "Got rather held up sorting out some papers with my boss in the office. He seems to think he owns me just because I'm his private secretary. I don't know why I should be telling you this, but I have threatened to quit if he is unable to respect my wishes to keep our office and private lives apart.

"Thank you for confiding in me like that," Alistair said with a lot of feeling.

"Would you like to come along with me and watch an amateur play? Our company has provided funds for its production – public relations, you see."

"Yes," Alistair said eagerly.

The play, 'Leather-Leathered' was about the flamboyant private life of a talented cricketer who wrecked his chance of playing for the West Indies cricket team when he suffered two black eyes and a broken nose in injuries inflicted on him with a cricket ball by his aggrieved ex-girlfriend, just before he was to fly out with the team for a summer tour of England. The play was staged in a school hall and was a pigeon-English verse drama in two acts by an avant-garde local poet and writer, Randy Richards; also well known for being a radical political activist and a cricket fanatic.

Lucy and Alistair sat in the back row of the school hall in a far corner. The audience was ecstatic, but Alistair found it all difficult to comprehend. He said to himself, "Could I really give a correct account of why I was here? Any such account would have to start, and perhaps end as well, with a consideration of the person sitting next to me: dear Lucy Berrt."

He moved a little closer to her. She was a very nice sort of person to be next to, even on the hard chairs of the school hall, though without having to strain his imagination perceptibly he found he could quite easily think up alternative and still more rewarding postures they might perhaps get into some time. More than once already he'd found his arm, as if demonically possessed, getting ready to move round her shoulders. He made it go back, but could tell it didn't want to. There were plenty of reasons, some of them perfectly harmless, why he and Lucy should console themselves for the thinness of the entertainment in the traditional way, but he knew they wouldn't appeal to her, or, being a woman, she'd pretend they didn't. Of course, there were one or two reasons on the other side as well, like the presence nearby of people who must know who she was.

Alistair pressed his knees firmly against hers. After fitting interval, and as if quite independently of his action, she shifted in her seat and moved her knee away. It wasn't, he said to himself, that she didn't like his knee – that wasn't it all. It was just that she wanted to give her full attention to the show, see?

"Aren't you getting a bit fed up with all this?"

The voice was Lucy's. Her utterance, which none in the whole semantic field could have incited him to a more profound assent, was delivered in a whisper so close to his ear that he felt her warm breath. How nice she really is, Alistair thought, how good and wise and brave and true. "Yes," he said.

"Come on, then."

He found himself following her between the line of knees and feet and the line of backs of heads. He knocked against a lot of the knees, trod on several of the feet, and without consciously willing it managed to deal almost every head a sharp cuff with his arm. There were loud sounds of protest, some from afar. "Sssh," Lucy said. A thunderous clank of iron pealed through the hall as she opened a side door. They got outside.

"We need a drink," Lucy said when they were in her car, then began disparaging 'Leather-Leathered.' Her remarks lacked cohesion or any basis in what some people used to call critical awareness, but they more than offset this by their violence and, here and there, picturesqueness. He hardly found it necessary to add a word. After a time, he said:

"If that's what you think about it, why did you ever get mixed up in it?"

"How do you mean?"

"Well, you had quite a bit to do with the production, didn't you? You must have seen some rehearsals."

"Yes, what about it?"

"Well… I can't see why you got mixed up in it." Alistair pursued.

"I've told you it was for the good image of the multinational corporation. You've got to support these things, you know."

"I can't see why. And wait a minute: weren't you the one who was telling me what a great poet Randy Richards was when we stood at the entrance of the school hall?"

"Oh, did I?" Lucy replied casually.

Alistair was silent for a moment. Then he said: "Walking out of his play won't encourage him much, will it?"

"That's quite different. You must see that."

"By what compulsion must I?"

"What? Stop arguing Alistair, can't you?"

They'd now arrived at her place. Alistair was still under mild sedation from seeing and hearing the 'Leather-Leathered.'

"Well, what have we come here for?" He asked with a glint in his eyes, as he got out of the car.

She gave a quick yap of laughter. "Well for a drink, I suppose, in the first instance."

Inside the house, they entered the living-room and Lucy got going at a cocktail cabinet mainly constructed of glass and chromium. Lucy handed him a drink and took him by the hand and sat him down beside herself on an opulent sofa. They had several drinks and some talk. She was looking very fine and was improved still further by the air of conscious dignity, existing with a slight threat of ludicrousness. She seemed to be enjoying herself, doing a fair amount of laughing and wriggling about a bit in her corner of the sofa.

Alistair sat there in an easy posture, his arm along the back of the sofa some inches from her shoulders, his head lolling comfortably. Was he now the man used to the company of attractive women, the man who accepts without dramatics whatever experience may come his way, but who never strives for anything beyond the bounds of expediency or of self-possession? This being so, it as odd that he had just started to tremble a little bit and to feel, on the whole, like a new boy at a large and prosperous school.

"I'd think I'd better be going," he said.

"Please yourself, Sir Galahad!"

She made no move to get up, but instead put down her glass and began staring at him, He felt as if he'd just been told he'd eaten carrion for tea. At last, she said: "What's eating you?"

He tried not to think of the last time they were together like this. "How do you mean?"

"You look like a man with a secret sorrow. What's the matter with you? What are you so gloomy about?"

"You've got me all wrong dear. I'm always full of fun. What you think me being gloomy is just… just that… I'm so much in love with you it hurts. Can't help it."

"Thank you, Alistair," she said, and gave him her steamiest, most seductive smile. She took his hand, and as she shifted her position, their bodies touched for an instant. A mutual thrill of desire raced through them.

"Later," she said softly. Alistair kept his hand on her waist long enough to feel her pliant flesh under her thin cotton dress. She looked up at him from the sofa, shaking her hair back Her eyebrows were arched as if in inquiry; her china-like teeth showed between her lips; her shoulders and breasts were heaving.

Alistair examined all this in an attempt to read there whether he should or should not go. It was little use; he might as well have scrutinized a cream bun for more imperatives or prohibitions.

She got up and put her arms round his neck. Wriggling a little, she leaned against him and tried kissing him, as a motorist on a cold morning might abandon the starter button and get going with the handle. He fired on the first swing and very soon they were swaying about, as if a gaucho had got them round the ankles with his lasso or bolas. Then they went and lay down on the sofa. Her clothes started to get seriously disarranged. After a while he said: "Wouldn't this be more fun in the bedroom?"

Just then the sound of an approaching car became audible, coming up her drive. Alistair felt as if he'd been suddenly deprived of some salient bodily organ, like heart or lungs. Lucy said: "Christ, I hope it's not Jerry again" and got up from the sofa.

"And who's Jerry?" Alistair asked, half-dreading the answer.

He'd been looking forward to an overall view of her nearly naked, but as things stood, he noticed little beyond the general fact. She ran to the window. "Yes, it's Jerry Hopkins my importunate boss, all right. Don't worry, I'll sort him out."

She began dressing with great dexterity and speed while Alistair watched her inattentively, the growing sound of the car in his ears. The car arrived under the window and its engine switched off.

"What does he want?" Alistair inquired.

"I expect he's come to apologise for his rude behaviour at the office today when I told him I had a date with someone special."

As she hurried out, one part of Alistair's mind listened intently to the sounds from below: footsteps on the stone walk, the front door opening, some raised voices in the hall, Lucy's laugh, silence. The other part of his mind wanted to find a place, perhaps one of the outer planets of Vega, where life at all levels was transmitted by asexual reproduction. Feet began mounting the stairs and approached the door of the lounge;

Alistair's mouth went drier. He looked up to the sound of female laughter. Lucy was alone. She gave another laugh standing with her feet apart and looking full of energy.

"The panics over Alistair. I accepted his apologies but told him I was handing in my notice all the same."

Suddenly Alistair knelt down before Lucy and asked: "Lucy, will you marry me?"

To his surprise she said 'Yes' as she hauled him up on to his feet and stood against him. "You seem surprised?"

"I shouldn't?"

"No. about five minutes after I met you at the party, I decided I was going to marry you, not just sleep with you."

"Can you explain?"

"No, I can't. Come on, let's go to the beach. We can no longer pick up here where we left off."

As they got to the beach in Lucy's sports car, there was some rhythmic toe-tapping calypso music vibrating from a nearby beach night club. Then they began to stroll across the soft sand towards the more remote corner of the bay. Alistair was feeling pretty contented and was enjoying the companionable silence between Lucy and himself when the calypso music was no longer audible.

Just ahead of them were two white nylon net hammocks, side by side, suspended between swaying lush palm trees close to the seashore. The moon was almost full, and a gentle breeze was blowing from the shimmering sea. Lucy broke the silence by saying: "Do you feel like a bathe?"

"Well," Alistair hesitated, feeling rather frightened or something. "I haven't got a costume."

"Neither have I. It doesn't matter, does it?"

"No, I suppose it doesn't."

"Nobody's likely to try and stop us. And it's still very warm."

This, at any rate was true, Alistair thought. He had begun to undress, vainly trying to keep sand away from the inside of his trousers. Lucy, unencumbered by shoelaces and socks, was quicker than he was and soon sauntered away towards the edge of the sea. He could see her quite clearly, a slightly hunched figure with her arms clasped round her breasts. The dry sand under the soles of his feet made a curious tickling. He walked up to Lucy and put an arm round her waist. She turned towards him and kissed him jovially.

Though she seemed to be shivering, she felt warm enough, as if she'd been rubbed with rough towels. When he tried to infuse something more personal than joviality into their embrace, she surprised him by leading him by the hand down the beach.

Why? Alistair wondered. What was there down there? Oh, of course, something had been said about a bathe, hadn't it? Well; dear Neptune! She must have been serious about it all the time, then.

After a few yards on terrible shingle, he could feel moisture underfoot. The waves were getting quite loud now and distinctly visible, and one of them darted forward and submerged his feet, Lucy instructed him to look at the phosphorescence caused by plankton in the water, Alistair was silent, standing still with his hands on his knees; a wave, unmarked by the usual band of white, slopped upwards over his wrists. He closed his eyes.

Wading nosily out to sea, Lucy pulled him after her, saying: "Come on in, it's wonderful, you'll feel marvelous when you come out."

He tried to get his brain to frame a sentence about it being all right for her with her thicker layer of subcutaneous fat, but it wouldn't.

"If I come out," he said instead, to which she coyly answered: "What?"

As a man burning to death will hurl himself blindly through a windowpane or over a stairhead he hurried after her, slipping and hurting his feet on the large stones, hardly noticing the titanic agony when the water reached his crotch, falling at last with scarcely a cry and going under the surface all over. After some minutes of oxygen-starvation, he found he was standing up to his chest in an element that, rightly considered, wasn't immediately lethal.

He waded towards Lucy, the water pouring itself against every inch of the submerged part of himself, and they kissed again. He ran his hand down her back and her flesh felt hard and marine, not like a person's, and her hair when it brushed his shoulder was like a sheaf of wet grass. He swam about for a bit, and then emerged onto the dry cold beach. He rubbed himself with his shirt and, priding himself on having thought of it, with his trouser-legs. Soon he felt less cold, and the sale started pricking and itching on his back.

Lucy began to talk, asking for and being granted the loan of his shirt, and saying how much she'd enjoyed the bathe. When Alistair was fairly dry, except for his hair, he went over to her. He could see the outlines of her shoulders and hips and breasts. "Come on, catch me if you can, let's have a go at those hammocks over there," she said playfully.

She got to her hammock before him and was already sitting in the middle of it with her legs stretched out in Alistair's path, trying to trip him up. He got into his and they began a mock fight to see who could dislodge the other from their hammock as they pushed hard with the soles of their feet, the branches of the palm trees swaying in sympathy.

Soon they both overbalanced and fell off their hammocks on to the beach sands. She laughed lightly and then stopped with an endearing lack of surprise when he took her by the arms and drew her down with him to a kneeling position on the sand. She got hold of what must have been her dress and spread it out. Close together, they lay on it side by side. Although the salt flaked lightly under his fingertips and faint runnels of moisture wandered from her hair, her flesh no longer felt hard or non-human, and although her arms and legs were cool, her body was warm again. Her face stayed wet and, in the darkness, couldn't sustain the self-will he'd seen on it. When her breathing became rapid it took on no strained shallowness.

There was something he didn't want to mention which he knew he had to mention. He mentioned it.

"It's all right, darling," she said in a blurred voice, "it doesn't matter with me honestly."

"Are you sure?"

"Yes, darling, oh yes…"

So at last, they did it. She moved about in his arms and then, with a sudden deep breath, went taut and still. Alistair could hear Lucy's voice mixed up with his own. She sighed and shifted her position. "That was good, wasn't it, darling?"

"Yes, it was good all right."

"You're quite a man, aren't you?"

"Oh, I don't know."

"Well, don't you love it?"

"Yes, I did then, but I love you more."

"And I love you very much."

They got up and began dressing. Alistair wondered how it was possible to ache so much and have so much sand on the body and inside the clothing without minding. With their arms round each other's waists, they walked back along the shore towards Lucy's car.

The following week they were married quietly in a Registry Office. Lucy was going to retain her maiden name and continue working in Barbados whilst Alistair went back to Perth. Jerry Hopkins had arranged for his own transfer back to New York after persuading Lucy to withdraw her resignation.

Six weeks later in a telephone call to Alistair, Lucy said excitedly: "I'm pregnant, Alistair. We are going to have a baby. Well, I'll be having it, not you."

"Pregnant! Lucy! Darling! You are sure? Are you all right?"

"Don't worry, I'm fine. Everything is under control. I intend to have the baby here in Barbados."

"I'll come right over. Are you sure you're all right?"

"Don't worry, darling. Take your time."

After the birth of their daughter at a private clinic near the Kensington Oval in Barbados, Lucy and the baby girl, Rachel, and Alistair flew out together to Scotland where Alistair had just bought a custom-built four-bedroom house on the outskirts of Perth.

Much later, Lucy had a tubal abortion when Rachel was two years old and she was not able to have any more children though she had dearly wished to have at least one other child.

Chapter 5

Rachel and I met when I was doing my first pre-registration house job in the professorial unit of a teaching hospital in Scotland. She had just qualified as a physiotherapist. I quickly warmed to her, not just because she was attractive and shapely, as most physiotherapists seemed to be, but mainly because of her winning ways with our most difficult patients and her dedication to her work.

Once again, I had forgotten what I came to do in the Resident's Office on seeing her move poetically past the office towards the wards. Her deportment was delightful. The other week I was dumbfounded when I became aware of her giving me a on serious look as if trying to sum me up.

I seemed to be repeatedly telling myself, "Forget about her and concentrate on you work, old chap." Added to that was a feeling that women were a thing in themselves that given the chance would make a not easily forgotten impression on me. Well, that was life, wasn't it? Yes, and especially this representative of that noteworthy sex. *That'll do, Desmond, that'll do, thank you. Give it a rest, can't you, Desmond?*

One morning, whilst I was again trying to exhort myself not to worry my head about Rachel as I dashed to take an emergency blood sample from a patient, I bumped into her at the door. It was my fault. I wasn't really looking where I was heading, for my thoughts were on … well, I just shouldn't let my thoughts wander, or rather sprint, in that direction. And besides, in the last few weeks I'd been enjoying myself no end, practicing the role of the truly strong man, the man superior to things like sex.

"I'm so sorry," I said, as I began to apologise profusely.

"Don't be silly, it was equally my fault," she said giving me a most amiable and heart-warming smile. "Dr. Smith," she continued, "my friend Stephanie has a birthday party on Saturday. Would you like to come?"

Luckily that was my weekend off. I lost no time in replying "Yes. Thank you. I would love to, very much."

"See you there and then," she said, smiling up at me. "Say, seven-thirty. Know the place?"

"I'll find out."

As I arrived at Stephanie's flat there was Rachel at the door to welcome me. She was dressed in a most gorgeous light blue taffeta dress with a discreet décolletage. She looked absolutely enchanting, radiant with a bewitching inner glow. There were a number of other doctors, nurses, and physiotherapist in the background as Stephanie handed round drinks, sausages, beef olives, crisps, biscuits, and nuts.

But I just seemed to be aware of only Rachel's presence and couldn't help peering down into her decolletage as she bent over to fetch a packet of twenty from her handbag. I felt an old and hateful excitement beginning to stir in me, the kind which, although mingled with apprehension, has the property of quickly casting off any hateful ingredient. In my medical school years, I'd spent a good deal of time and energy in courting and avoiding that excitement. Dear, dear. I wanted to shut my eyes: there are some things a man doesn't like to see unprepared. I sweated a little, or at any rate felt convinced that I ought to, and started praying for and against interruption. This was once provided when Stephanie came round offering me more drinks and sausages and potato crisps.

Rachel soon straightened herself up. She placed a cigarette between her thin lips, snapped her lighter, lit the cigarette slowly, inhaled and blew out smoke, she offered me one.

"No thanks, Rachel, I don't."

"Wise man," she said.

"And by the way, Rachel, do call me Desmond from now on; Dr. Smith is common enough."

"All right, Desmond. Now, would you care for a dance?"

"My pleasure, but I'm positively hopeless at dancing; probably tread on your toes all the time."

"Doesn't matter. I'm no good either."

Apart from the disco music we also had rock 'n' roll, quick-step and samba. Rachel turned out to be a good dancer and I soon began enjoying myself. There was too much noise to speak much, but the bodily contact with her had its own appeal. I could see that there was a lot to be said for dancing as a way of getting one's arms round girls and so on. Like all attractive women, Rachel was somehow more attractive close to than at a distance.

This was brought home to me with extra force when, after a few minutes, she laid her cheek on mine. She continued, however, to dance with accuracy, not sacrificing her freedom of movement by pressing or leaning against me. Her agility made her seem even slimmer and harder than I first imagined. When she moved her face away, I saw that she had a very good jaw-line, smoothly fleshed but firm and straight.

"I have a confession to make," she suddenly said.

"Yes?"

"The incident at the door when we bumped into each other that morning wasn't entirely an accident. No, not really. I could have avoided it if I wanted to."

"Explain yourself, Rachel."

"Come on. Let's have another dance," she said playfully.

"I wondered if a certain basic human activity ever entered her thoughts, or was there all the time. Perhaps she was a little devil when she was roused? I soon asked her: "Do you mind if I walk you to your bus-stop?"

"I was wondering if you were ever going to ask, Desmond."

Just before the party wound to an end we took our leave of Stephanie, thanking her for the lovely time we had and the good feed.

As we walked in silence to the side street where her bus-stop was, she pulled me into a shadow, put her arms around my neck and began kissing me. When I responded she opened her mouth, then caught my hand and laid it on her breast. Her heart was going quickly as she bit my tongue a little too hard. We became locked in an ardent embrace. The tips of my fingers trailed from her hair to her shoulders and then on to her breasts and between her legs and back to her full, high breasts; this time the tips hardened as if by magic. *So beautiful!* Tenderly, tentatively, I bent low to cup her breasts as they heaved. She sighed and then shuddered, Slowly, she began to tidy herself up.

"I must go now, Desmond," she said in a shaky voice.

Six months late, towards the end of my preregistration year, Rachel invited me up to Perth to see her parents. I stayed the weekend there with Rachel and her parents and a month later Rachel and I were engaged.

After a year, when I settled in a surgical job in Farnham, Surrey, we married and went to Barbados for our honeymoon.

Though we had managed to save a bit between us before our marriage, this was apparently not enough on the junior doctor's pay I was on to secure us the mortgage for the house we wanted. It was a semi-detached, not far from Farnham Castle and the Bush Hotel. Rachel's father insisted on 'loaning' us the balance as a marriage present.

Nine months after we moved into the house, our daughter, Anne, was born. She was a happy child, and no trouble at all, sleeping most of the night so long as she was left to sleep on her stomach. She was a great joy to us, and Rachel's life seemed to revolve around her to such an extent that I sometimes felt she was enjoying twisting Rachel around her little finger.

The only sour note was that Rachel had wanted me to be there at her birth, but I was called out to deal with an emergency admission at the time. Somehow, she still thought I should have arranged a cover and made sure I was there at Anne's birth – no so easy, as I tried to explain, when you are on a one-in-two rota and never quite sure when the baby will decide to come into the world.

Chapter 6

When Anne was a few months old she had a canine friend, a Jack-Russell puppy called Jimmy. She had seen a Jack-Russell dog from her pram darting around in the park, chasing dogs twice his size, and Anne got all excited, pointing repeatedly at the dog.

Anne and Jimmy – or "Dimmy' as she called him – grew up together and became devoted friends. She would cry "Leave Dimmy alone!" if he was being banished to his basket for being naughty. Jimmy enjoyed being stroked by Anne who would not infrequently pull his ears and his docked tail and put her hands in his mouth and Jimmy wouldn't yelp, bark, or do anything to hurt her; at most he just backed away to hide under a sofa or something. Especially when she was very young, Jimmy often kept watch by Anne's bed and if any strangers came near would growl and snarl at them.

He took a little while to get house trained and, though he was very protective and forbearing towards Anne, he had an admirable self-esteem, and would not brook being pushed around by any other person, including Rachel and me, unless he was feeling and looking guilty for having done something he knew he shouldn't have done. He was also intolerant of most strangers unless somehow, he sensed they were not afraid of him or some inexplicable empathy was established between him and the stranger at first sight and encounter.

He was generally no problem, so long as he had his long walk and exchanged sniffy messages with other dogs along the way and had his feed. Otherwise, he got very frisky and played all manner of tricks to get attention, his favourite being to snatch Anne's dolls or playthings, clutching them in his powerful jaws and daring you to come get them. And the rascal could be more cunning than a prison rat the way he could hide his favourite things, especially food, in remote corners of the house and garden.

Jimmy, once he got his teeth into anything, would never let go unless diverted. As the dog grew older the postman learnt to keep his distance from him and spent the minimum time possible trying to pop letters through our letterbox.

"That youngster never seems to mellow with age," the postman once and again muttered under his breath.

How Jimmy invariably knew when the postman was approaching the house, even when he must have been more than twenty yards from the house and there was plenty of masking traffic noise, I never could tell. He had been taken to the vet and neutered, but he was back to his old self after a couple of months.

The wonderful thing about dear Jimmy was that he had plenty of guts and character and was a good trier. I don't think he was the most amenable house dog – he often had to be put away in an upstairs bedroom when visitors came and his behaviour became insupportable, but then he occasionally retaliated by peeing on a favoured patch of the carpet – he was most loyal. If

I were unexpectedly detained at work, he would sit and wait by the door at the exact time I would normally be back.

Fairly early on he began to despise and turn up his nose at proprietary dog foods, much preferring to have a taste of what we ourselves were eating. He was particularly partial to spaghetti, bacon ad bacon rinds, cheese biscuits, grilled meat chop drippings, and of course the chops themselves, given half the chance. He had a variable taste for sardines.

When he got knocked down by a reckless cyclist in the park, when Anne was five years old, and had to be put down because of his severe injuries, Anne was inconsolable. She sobbed herself to sleep calling: "Dimmy, Dimmy, my Dimmy." She wanted to join 'Dimmy' wherever it was that dogs went when they were no longer with us.

Chapter 7

We left Farnham after two years and moved to London, followed by moves to Oxford and then to Nottingham in the usual merry-go-round of NHS junior hospital doctors in training, chasing after the next senior appointment in their specialty – uprooting their family with each move.

When Anne was six years old, we took her on a three-week Italian trip, stopping off in Rome, Naples, and Venice. Rome was an assault on the senses, and this began the moment we arrived. It seemed like a living, vibrant museum with its 2000-year-old past stamped all over its modern twentieth century face.

Everything was nosier and larger than life. The horn-honking traffic was devastating as it bumped over the cobbles of the main piazzas, testy policemen tried hopelessly to control it, taxis lurched on two wheels round the 'Wedding Cake' monument to Vittorio Emanuele revving up under the window from which Mussolini used to wave to the crowd. We could almost hear the roar of the tens of thousands of excited spectators as we stood among the ruins of the Colosseum…

'We who are about to die, salute you'... the gladiators with their swords, their tridents... the hungry lions and the frightened little Christian girls facing them, expecting gruesome death at any moment...

Wherever we wondered we saw some antiquity or other; a Corinthian pillar propping up a new supermarket, an ornate fountain as we rounded a corner, a half-forgotten church. Modern city life just carried on around it. Only the tourists were impressed.

We walked most of the time, carrying Anne now and again but she was a good walker and entered entirely into the spirit of the adventure. We followed the Tiber as it snaked like a muddy worm through to the Vatican City where every visitor, and almost the whole of Rome seemed to turn out on a Sunday morning, except, we gathered, during the summer months. At the stroke of midday on the Sunday morning we found ourselves in St. Peter's Square, the Pope emerged at a far-corner window of this top-storey apartment to give us and a throng of other visitors his papal blessing.

We spent almost a whole day in the Vatican City visiting St. Peter's, the Vatican Museums and gazing up at Michelangelo's ceiling in the Sistine Chapel. After the colosseum and the Vatican City we went to the Forum – where one hardly needed a fertile imagination to complete the jigsaw of standing arches and columns to give a photofit picture of how it all started. We walked down the Spanish Steps and then went to the Pantheon whose old massive metal doors plus the still functional marvel of its original drainage system made one salute the genius of the ancient Romans.

On top of Rome's smallest hill, we went to the Capitoline Museums crammed full of magnificent sculptures like the 'Dying Gaul' and 'Romulus, Remus, and the She-Wolf.'"

When the roar of the traffic and the constant overture of the horns became too much, we climbed up the Palatine Hill. Past the Forum, walked in the Borghese Gardens and wandered around the Protestant Cemetery where the graves of Keats and Shelley lay in relative calm.

We treated Anne to scrumptious ice creams in the Piazza Navona. Then we wandered around the old quarter of Trastevere where the streets where so narrow that the balconies almost touched each other. In a very old Roman restaurant here, we were served Abbacchio (roast lamb) and Saltimbocca Alla Romana (veal escalopes with ham and sage). There were quite a few tourists in the restaurant including a couple of Japanese. Unfortunately, the manager of the restaurant appeared to be pulling a fast one on the tourists by making up hugely inflated unitemised bills scrawled in an illegible hand. To our surprise the two Japanese men brought out their pocket calculators at the same time, did some computing, and muttered something to each other. They then leaned over to the customer sitting close to them on an adjacent table, still tapping away at their calculators, and said something. All three seemed to nod their heads in concert. With great briskness the Japanese left what they calculated their bills should have been on their side plates got up and left.

"Bully for you!" I said under my breath.

The erstwhile simpering and rather podgy restaurant manager wasn't very amused. Neither were we as we settled up as billed and left the restaurant convinced we had been overcharged, but resolved never to eat there again.

The next day we went window-shopping in the Vias Condotti and Sistina. I deliberately kept a discreet distance from Rachel to avoid being lured by her into the shops – the prices there made you howl with pain. From the Via Nazionale we went to the somewhat cramped area around the Trevi fountains. There Anne threw a few coins over her left shoulder as a token of her desire to come back to Rome!

A few days later we went up north to Venice, 'La Serenissima,' once the heart of a rich empire. I fell in love with it at first sight, and it happened to be my birthday the day we arrived. I felt there was no place on earth and water like Venice, built, we were told, on 114 islets, crisscrossed by 177 canals, spanned by 459 bridges and lapped by the waves of the island-dotted lagoon.

As soon as we had been shown to our rooms in a hotel close to the main Railway Station and the Grand Canal, we set out to explore the city at leisure. Venice was, indeed, an unrivalled treasure-house of art and architecture, of stunning beauty and opulent flamboyance, of dedicated piety and voluptuous ostentation, of the good and the bad – but never the dull, it seemed.

A maze of canals, streets, alleys, and squares were lined by ornate and at times, alas, decaying buildings. There were no vehicles to knock us down, although a hurrying Venetian elbowed us aside as we walked over the shop-lined Rialto Bridge that spanned the Grand Canal. We learned that Shylock did business here! On the other side of the bridge we meandered through very narrow streets and alleys to reach the magnificent St. Marks Square, apparently known to the Venetians simply as 'Piazza.' After exploring the mysterious Byzantine interior of the multi-domed cathedral, Rachel and I had coffee in the Square whilst Anne had some ice cream as well as great fun and excitement running after the pigeons. We had a splendid pasta lunch at a nearby canopied trattoria before taking the lift to the top of the 320-foot-high bell tower, the Capanile, where we enjoyed the finest panoramic view of the city and lagoon.

The next day, we hired a gondola for an hour and glided gently along the canals as the straw-hatted gondolier serenaded Anne. She was thrilled to bits. However, towards the end she began to retch and feel sick. We had planned to have a ride on one of the waterbuses, 'vaporetti,' but had to go back to the hotel as soon as we got off the gondola. Back at the hotel she looked rather unwell; she had a slight temperature and said her throat hurt. I looked inside her throat and it was moderately inflamed. She was put to bed and given some paracetamol syrup and fluids. Two days later she was back to her old sprightly self. As a treat for her, the following day we took her to the sun, sea, and sand of the Venice Lido after a fifteen-minute water-bus ride across the lagoon to the Lido's central landing stage. She was in high spirits as she built her sandcastles and collected an assortment of seashells in a white plastic bag.

And when we got back home from Italy, she confided that the messing around on the Lido beach was by far the most enjoyable part of the trip for her.

A couple of days later we headed south to Naples and the Neapolitan Riviera, 'The Divine Coast,' via Monte Cassino, the beautifully restored Benedictine monastery which commands an entrancing view of the Liri Valley. On the map the Riviera didn't look up to much, a gnarled rather stubby finger of land poking into the Mediterranean, segregating the Gulf of Naples from the Gulf of Salerno.

Naples itself, especially the city centre with its fountains, grand buildings, parks with blazing flower beds, and palm-lined avenues, was vibrant with life, if chaotic. The streets and alleyways of Old Naples were so narrow that the balconies almost touched each other, and with the washing hanging over most of the balconies they actually did seem to touch. After an overnight stop, we drive along the spectacular sweep of palm-studded bay, past the Lover's Fountain. We stopped over at Pompeii on our way to Sorrento.

An 'expert' local guide accompanied us around the excavations at Pompeii destroyed in 79AD by the eruption of the volcano Vesuvius and preserved by the ashes; it all brought history poignantly to life. Apparently, most of the cataclysmic ash was belched up one afternoon as the Pompeiians were in the throes of campaigning for secret ballot elections. Preserved on some of the walls were electoral inducements and propaganda. It also seemed as if quite a few of the Pompeiians did manage to escape being buried alive by the volcanic ash.

Wheeled traffic in downtown Pompeii seemed to have been well regulated and directed, the ruts sunk in the cobbled streets (especially of the marketplace) by the vehicle wheels are still clearly visible; intact, or nearly intact, stepping stone blocks, around which the wheels of the vehicles skirted, were set in the main streets and allowed pedestrians to cross the garbage-strewn thoroughfares in relative safety and comfort.

The type of dwelling, house or villa reflected the social status of the owner... In the big houses and villas, it seemed the servants lived upstairs, whilst their masters were ensconced downstairs, the floor of the living-rooms sloping towards the centre and the door nearest the patio to allow easy sluice-down of the results of their food and drink indulgences as they reclined on their couches; at the entrance to one of the big houses was the warning 'Beware of Dogs'... the water-storage tanks of the storeyed houses and the original plumbing systems looked in reasonable condition... The shops and stalls had sliding doors... There were foreign exchange booths here and there in the marketplace... Wine stalls were plentiful and were strategically placed along the main market streets... Drinking fountains abundant and the joints of the connecting lead pipes were still basically sound... There was a sundial clock near the Forum which could still tell reasonably accurate time... There were some 'time-frozen' stone-hard bodies of the victims of the eruption encased in volcanic ash...

The explicit pornographic drawings and paintings in the private downstairs rooms of the mostly restored patio villas of two rich bachelor merchants will take a lot of beating even by modern sexually liberated standards; one of the chaps even commissioned an artist to draw him weighing his greatly exaggerated penis on a creaking lop-sided golden balance.

Anne pointing to one of the drawings shouted, to our embarrassment: "What are those funny people, the man and the woman, doing without their clothes on, mummy?"

Basic human concerns and pursuits don't seem to have changed much over the centuries.

From Pompeii we drove to within a few hundred feet of the peak of the volcano Vesuvius. There was a decided smell of rotten eggs in the ambient air. We didn't feel inclined to walk up to the crater's edge, especially with Anne in tow. After having some Spaghetti al Pomodoro in a local restaurant, we traveled on to Sorrento.

The birds' eye panorama from the clifftop 'corniche' road simply stole my breath away, as we wound round the stretch of corkscrew road that led to Sorrento. The Scenery of the Neapolitan Rivera was natural in the wildest sense of the word. The great limestone peninsula looked eroded into every shape but loose – though discreet curtains of net have been erected to catch the occasional falling morsels of rock. The rock, here and there with a generous topsoil of volcanic ash, in no way equaled a landscape of stark severity. All but the sheerest surfaces were covered with a blanket of vegetation: vineyards, pinewoods, citrus and olive groves, almond trees, camellias, oleanders and countless other blooms. Here the dividing line between wilderness and man-tamed garden was almost impossible to draw.

The buildings of the coast were all of two colours – white or every shade of confetti and they simply cascaded down the mountain sides, settling around a church or cathedral and then slid on into the sea.

We arrived at Sorrento, perched above its harbours, in the evening. It offered stunning views over a magnificent stretch of the coast of the Bay of Naples. Villas, hotels, and cafes spread out on either side of the town, sweeping down to the resort's small beaches and the shimmering blue waters of the sea.

The town's winding alleyways and quaint streets were honeycombed with stalls and boutiques offering everything from fashionable clothes to simple pleasant handicraft. Public transport seemed good – boats, trains, and buses. A couple of 'Torna a Sorrento!' leaflets were slipped into our carrier-bag as we left a leather-goods shop with a couple of purchases.

We had supper in the hotel restaurant and sampled some excellent seafood dishes – 'Sarde a Beccafico:' sardines stuffed with a mouthwatering mixture of breadcrumbs, garlic, parsley, cheese, and capers; steaks of swordfish; tuna cooked 'alla brace' and served with a dressing of oil and lemon. For sweets we had delicately coloured ice-creams and lemon sorbets.

We could only stay two nights in Sorrento before returning to Britain via Rome Ciampino airport, slightly earlier than planned, because Anne was beginning to feel unwell again.

Chapter 8

When we came back from Italy Rachel was in such a radiant and amorous mood that the night after our return, she surprised me by giving me her steamiest come-hither smiles and saying seductively in bed:

"I feel like having another baby. Right now, I desire you utterly and I want all your desire."

We made love a couple of times that night passionately and beautifully. The embarrassing quality of this avowal made me start thinking things over afterwards. It had been sometime since she 'desired' me, whether utterly or not, without a long prelude on my part of arduous and even undignified badgering and pursuit. One often had to lay out indefinite reserves of tact and ingratiation in order to stay 'desired.'

Someone once said that the fundamental problem with each of us is the rest of us. Human relationships are at once at the root of most of our problems and the essence of all our glorious achievements.

As Rachel increasingly and single-mindedly sought what she called 'self-realization,' it looked as if we were now engaged in an undeclared competition and battle of wills. This assumed different guises at different times.

"But do we have a divine right to guard our own interest at all costs?" I remember once asking her in the heat of an argument. "A divine right to isolated independency?" I continued.

I suggested that perhaps humanity was only complete when male and female were together and the keynote was mutuality, and that even the Book of Genesis the only part of Creation pronounced 'not good' -was the alone-ness of man. Got it all wrong again?

I said to myself "Well, I think I've tried my level best to understand her moods and standpoint as far as it is humanely possible for me to do, but I seem to have failed miserably." I suppose the disruption of our family life by my on-call schedules and the frequent house moves with each job change in the NHS did not help matters. And when Anne died on her seventh birthday after her life support machines had been switched off, the affectionate conjugal relationship between us was, it seemed, switched off at the same time. And so we separated. But I still loved Rachel. How much I was now rather uncertain.

Soon afterwards I got a job as a temporary Consultant Surgeon near when we lived and moved out into a flat. Rachel resumed her career as a physiotherapist.

Chapter 9

I became restless, and a seed-thought in my mind for a total change of scene became a full-grown intention to got to Saudi Arabia and the Middle East when I came across an advert in one of the leading British medicinal journals in the overseas section.

I had been on a long walk to get myself sorted out, to take stock and lay plans, and the fresh air seemed to have provided the inspiration I needed. I can well understand 'Life' being allegorized into a walk in John Bunyan's *Pilgrim's Progress*. A walk seems to minister to so many moods – a delectable madness but very good for sanity.

One often walks to make a virtue out of necessity, though constitutionals and leisurely perambulation can be made creative use of. During the walk I was able to see my peck of troubles in some perspective as my thoughts passed through long tunnels of darkness and I was uncertain whether there would be light at the end. I was seeking a thread of hope and promise to cling to in the darkness. Perhaps there is a purpose in every seeming disaster which may just be another piece in the jigsaw of growth in life?

Perhaps over possessiveness is really the root of all evil and conflicts? – the love of money, over possessiveness over our virtues, ideas, group egos, and in our relationships. Is it a form of insecurity? I suppose an acid test of security is vulnerability: on admission of mistakes. However, we can't really possess love, ideas, and similar things – they're are bigger than we are? We can only reflect on them? Perhaps we can merely reflect and use the good things of life without the fruitless determination to own them? Perhaps what in the end we possess is our own character, acquired through many choices?...

When I got back to my flat, I phoned a number of companies in London with interests in recruiting medical personnel for Saudi Arabia and the Middle East. They asked for my curriculum vitae and photocopies of my professional certificate. A month later I was invited to attend two interviews, one in Grosvenor Gardens the other near Park Lane. It took another six weeks before I heard from them. Both companies wrote to say that the outcome of the interviews for a Consultant Surgeon post had been favourable: when would I be ready to travel? One appointment was for the United Arab Emirates and the other for Saudi Arabia.

I chose to go to Saudi Arabia simply because the tax-free remuneration was more attractive, though social life was probably going to be tougher and more restrictive there. Well, few people seemed to go to those parts for more than the financial reward.

After going through an elaborate medical examination in Harley Street and signing the contract for the job in Saudi Arabia at the London office of the company near Park Lane, I resigned my temporary Consultant Surgeon post. The company got on with the process, sometimes inexplicably prolonged, of getting me my visa and work permit; I was scheduled to fly out to Jeddah from London Heathrow with Saudia Airlines in four weeks.

Chapter 10

A couple of days before I was due to leave, I had a telephone call from the company in London to say that I was to fly to Dhahran instead of Jeddah – on a British Caledonian flight. I was needed urgently at a recently opened multi-billion royal military hospital named after one of the Saudi kings. Yes, my appointment had been approved by the Ministry of Defence and Aviation (MODA); no, my entry visa was not yet ready; yes, I should collect my passport with my visa and work permit at Gatwick airport on the morning of the departure; no, there was no map of Saudi Arabia available that showed where the military hospital was, but the hospital wasn't 'too far' from Al-Khobar; yes, someone from the London office of the company would be at Gatwick airport not only to meet me but also introduce me to three other doctors who would be traveling with me: A Belgian gynecologist and obstetrician from Brussels, Dr. Peter Jacobs; an Irish Consultant anesthetist from Dublin, Dr. Frank O'Neill; and a Dutch Consultant pediatrician from Amsterdam, Dr. Paul van Waveren.

On the day of the departure, I arrived in good time at Gatwick airport from Victoria Station. I had intended to travel light but decided at the last moment to take a couple reference textbooks with me just in case, as I wasn't sure what there was at the hospital. This, I soon found out, was to cost me dear though I was much later on reimbursed by the company.

There was some difficulty and delay in tracing my passport in the upstairs offices of British Caledonian Airways mainly because the Arabic travel agency that booked my flight had put a slightly different name on the buff-coloured padded envelope containing my passport and other documents. When it was finally found, after rechecking with the agency I had just enough time to check in and board the plane.

When I looked at my ticket on checking in, I discovered that my baggage allowance was anything but generous and that I had quite a few kilos of excess baggage to pay for. I had put the textbooks in my main luggage suitcase; perhaps I should have put at least one of them in my shoulder bag. Well, it set me back a tidy sum and there was not time to do anything but pay up, otherwise I would have missed the plane. *Not a good start*, I thought.

On the way to board the plane I met up with the three traveling companions I had been told about: Dr. Peter Jacobs, Dr. Frank O'Neill, and Dr. Paul van Waveren; but I never met the company representative. Peter, Frank, Paul, and I soon formed a small circle of firm friends at the hospital, usually going for walks and shopping trips together, mostly on Fridays. We more often than not shared the same table in the dining room.

We took off on time. I had a window seat in a non-smoking compartment. As we got near the Saudi frontier alcoholic beverages were no longer permitted. I sat with my nose very nearly pressed to the double-layered glass as I looked down from the sky at the desert below. The landscape was barren. I squinted in the sun's glare. Below us was a desolate wilderness of sand, gravel, and gullies. I looked from the dreary humps of bare brown hills to the drearier stretches of lifeless black lava-land. I consulted my watch and yawned.

Dhahran was still some hours away, on the far side of this desert, to the east along the Gulf that used to be called Persian and now had chauvinistically been renamed 'Arabian' by the Saudis. I shook my head. Below us was still Jordan, I thought.

Some of the Arabs in the plane wearing long white Saudi robes and head scarves were staring disapprovingly at a young American couple as the girl threw her arms around the man and started kissing him on the lips. The man had shot a quick, cautious glance around the cabin to see if any of the Arabs sitting nearby were watching them; then he reached over and took the girl's hand in his. Possessively he fingered her wedding ring. Tenderly he stroked her hand. He wished there was some way he could insulate her from the inevitable shocks of the next hours and days and weeks as they looked forward to their shared camp-site life in Aramco. For their honeymoon, she insisted on coming out with him to Aramco where he had been working for the past three years as a construction engineer and had managed to make quit e a bit of money during the period.

He has told her may times what to expect, but often he had wondered if she had really listened. In Saudi she would have to adjust to a sudden and overwhelming denial of the personal freedom she was used to in Southern California. She wouldn't, for instance, be allowed to drive a car. He sighed. He held her hand more tightly to reassure her. She then turned and smiled at him before throwing her arms around him to kiss him on the lips as she remembered their honeymoon in Europe. There he had put his arm around her as they strolled through the dark romantic streets of Florence. He had kissed her under the lamp posts in Paris. And in their favourite place of all, in gloriously schmaltzy Vienna, he had scarcely been able to keep his hands off her.

Now she was transported back to the night of their secret wedding after they eloped to get married at a rural hamlet. She, Kathy Jordon, had stood beside Robert Presley as the Justice of the Peace cleared his throat and asked again if anyone knew of any reason why these two should not be married.

The old man had recited this brief service in the hamlet for nigh on thirty-five years. He was accustomed to young couples who wanted desperately to share a bed as man and wife. Well, they had their marriage license though Kathy was more nervous than most brides. They were there of their own of their free will. They had that lovers' glow that his wife and his sister-in-law, pressed into their usual duty as witnesses, always found so romantic. This was a quickie wedding like maybe a thousand others he had performed, and so he stifled a yawn and continued on with the service.

They recited their vows, and the Justice of the Peace pronounced them man and wife. Kathy was twenty and Robert twenty-nine. Her father, Gary, was a property developer in California and she was now his only child since her brother, John and mother, Ellen, were killed in a car crash when she was sixteen. Her father had become very protective towards her – she thought stiflingly overprotective – and had gone out of his way to provide her, with much lavishness, practically all she wanted materially, including a purebred Arabian horse on her seventeenth birthday.

She was the most gloriously beautiful chestnut horse Kathy had ever seen – a large, high-spirited, copper-coloured horse with a luxuriant black mane of hair and huge tender eyes and a swishing black tail. Kathy had started in rapt astonishment at her dream come true: an Arabian horse just like those in the picture books.

"So, what do you think of her?" Asked Miss Paton, who ran a riding academy nearby, and had been Kathy's riding instructor since her early teens. "When your father asked me if I could get the horse for you I picked this one out in Virginia," Miss Paton explained. "Believe me, Kathy, this mare is the best there is."

"She's a beauty, don't you think?" Her father had asked proudly.

Kathy continued to stare with saucer eyes at the magnificent horse. She opened her mouth to ask if the gorgeous creature was really an Arabian, but her voice came out as a wordless squeak.

"Take a closer look," Miss Paton urged her.

With reverent hesitation Kathy approached the horse, which was hands higher than any she had ever ridden. The mare had a thicker neck, a broader ribcage, more muscular quarters. And remembering what she had read once about this breed, Arabians had larger hearts than any other horses in the world.

Shyly Kathy had smiled up at the horse. Books had prepared her for the size and stature of an Arabian, but not for how very pretty its face could be. This mare had long pointy ears, a dainty muzzle, flaring nostrils, and eyes that were too intelligent and human to belong to a mere animal.

"Happy birthday, honey," her father hugged her.

Kathy edged reverently closer to the most beautiful horse who had the best bloodlines in the world. When, finally, she had stood in front of the horse, the mare inclined her head and seemed to be studying the girl. Then the horse shook her proud head and whinnied.

"She LIKES me!" Kathy reached up on her tiptoes, and when the mare dropped her head, Kathy threw her arms around her neck. The horse nuzzled her.

That year Kathy met Robert Presley at a disco party in San Francisco that she had attended against her father's will. Robert had started studying oil engineering and technology at a graduate school in Texas before transferring to a college in California where he completed his studies. Kathy's father did not approve of their relationship; he thought Robert's occupation 'rough,' and had plans, of his own for her to be friendly with and eventually marry Charles Barkley, the son of a business partner, who'd just graduated from the Harvard Law School.

Robert had gone to Saudi Arabia to work for the Arabian-American Oil Company, or Aramco. Toward the end of the war, Standard Oil of California, the largest stock owner in the original Saudi oil concession, needed capital to gear up for a massive postwar boom. High-level corporate American wheeling and dealing resulted in Texaco, Jersey Standard, and Mobil becoming partners in the oil-concession cartel that was renamed the Arabian-American Oil Company.

And that was only the beginning. During the wartime oil-production cutbacks, American wives, children, and all unessential personnel had been sent home, so that there had been fewer than two thousand Americans left in Dhahran. But by the summer of 1948, there were at least eight thousand in residence. Besides the oilmen, hundreds of construction workers had been imported to build everything from bunkhouses, schools, and a hospital, to roads and even swimming pools. Most of the original pioneers had come there not only for the high pay but for a love of adventure and the thrill of surviving life on the edge. Latter-day Aramco employees like Robert came fully briefed on the brutal climate and the isolation and monotony of living a restricted life inside a sequestered compound. To recruit and hold its staff, Aramco paid them at least twenty percent more than Texas oil companies. It was said that if Americans could 'stick it out' in Saudi for twenty years, they could retire to Florida as millionaires. To sweeten the pot, Aramco offered not only high salaried and lavish vacations but a lifestyle that did its best to replicate a quiet suburb in Southern California.

But as the gap in living standards between Americans and Arabs began to widen in Saudi, there was even less mixing between the two nationalities than in the pioneer times. American oilmen and their wives dressed up in their summer whites and dined and danced by the country-clubby pool at the Patio. Steaks and eggs and every other Western taste delight were shipped in from Australia and sold in the company commissary. Bevies of single American women worked as secretaries and lived on shady streets know as Petticoat Lane and Virgin Circle. Butt part of the price for Aramco's attempt to create a Little America there in the Saudi desert was that life in Dhahran was artificial and hollow and rife with contradictions.

Robert came to the Aramco compound in Dhahran not only to establish himself financially but also to get over the emotional trauma of his frustrated relationship with Kathy whose father was determined to see that nothing came of it and had explicitly warned him to desist from trying to see her again. But although Kathy did not dislike Charles, she did not love him.

She managed secretly to keep in touch with Robert by letters and telephone calls, and when he came back this year on his vacation, they decided to elope and get married.

After the Justice of the Peace had pronounced them man and wife, and they had kissed each other briefly, they left for a quaint and venerable inn a few miles away. The bespectacled innkeeper studied the seal on their marriage certificate and after making Robert pay in advance, he booked them in.

While Robert went back to the front desk to see about some supper, Kathy remained in their room. She looked out the wide windows at blooming flower beds and rolling pastures and forested hills. Then she sank down on the deep softness of massive double bed covered by a handmade patchwork quilt. She could not resist bouncing once or twice, as a child will just for joy. She considered peeling off her clothes and greeting him stark naked upon his return. She was eager for her first real experience of sex.

She had been groped familiarly a couple of time before at parties and she had now almost forgotten the boy next door who had pulled down her knickers to touch her dampness between her legs; the agreeable sensation it aroused; however, she had not forgotten. She wanted to be so uninhibited and passionate that Robert would never dream of touching any other woman again.

To prepare for tonight, she had read some purple passages including D. H. Lawrence's 'Lady Chatterley's Lover,' although she had been shocked more by the coarse language than by what the gamekeeper did to the lady after he threw her repeatedly to the floor or the ground. Kathy smoothed down the quilt on her marriage bed. She knew what to expect. The earth would move. It would be like crescendos of symphonic music washing over her, like waves beating on the shore, like trumpets sounding and bells ringing all the dreams she had ever dreamt all instantaneously coming true. The ecstasy of it would make her swoon into unconsciousness. She could hardly wait! She knew she was just going to love sex!

Yet when Robert strode into their dining room without knocking, she was still demurely sitting on the edge of the bed her knees pressed tightly together, wearing all her clothes. She waited expectantly for him to tear those clothes off her. But when he merely told her they would have to go down to the dining room to eat, she put on her jacket and followed him out the door. First, they would eat; then they would come together in that nice big bed. He praised the heartiness of her appetite at dinner.

At last they were back in the room together. She took a quick shower, she put on her frilly white nearly transparent negligee, she struck a pose framed in the window with moonlight washing over her so he would be tantalized by the outline of her body. He pulled back the sheets of the bed and slowly discarded all of his clothes as she stood breathlessly watching him. Then he beckoned to her, and she ran to him and felt his naked skin through the thin nightgown.

He kissed her on the lips until she was dizzy; then he kissed her throat until she was faint. He kissed her shoulders and pulled her negligee down and kissed her breasts. Slowly he slid the nightgown to her waist and then her hips, and when he finally let it fall to the floor, he held her to him and kissed her and the erotic thrill of flesh against flesh coursed through them. They sank down on the bed, and he kissed her and held her and told her again and again he loved her.

As his hands and then his mouth found her breasts, she flushed in the chest and neck and face. The tip of his tongue on the nipples of her breasts was as gentle as though she were not a woman but a delicate tropic flower that would wilt from rough handling. Passion, he thought, as he adored her with his tongue, could come later, on the eternity of nights and afternoons and mornings of their loving.

For an exquisitely long time, he stroked her from her breasts over her soft rounded belly to her knees, then he parted her legs and touched her until she moaned. Finally he whispered endearment to her as he slowly lowered himself on her and pushed through her membrane and was finally home inside her. Over and over, he said her name, he continued to kiss her.

He drew out his loving long enough for her to recover from the initial shock and slight pain of his entry, and she could begin to think that he felt good, although filling her up. If the earth did not exactly move for Kathy, if symphonies did not quite sound, if the slightest little quiver of orgasm never quite shook her, still this first time with Robert was warm and sweet and loving.

When he began to shake with his own climax, she did not understand what was happening. Instinctively she wrapped her legs around his buttocks and folded her arms and the essence of herself even closer around him. When his shuddering stopped, she crooned to him. She stroked his hair and felt utterly at peace and at one with all the forces of light in the world.

She wanted only to lie naked in his arms and drift blissfully off to sleep but Robert bounded out of bed and into the bathroom to take a brisk shower.

"You see," came Robert's distant voice, "in Saudi Arabia all good Muslims, they say, think it unmanly, even unhealthy, to fall asleep with all those sexual juices still flowing unwashed between couples."

Lying alone on the crumpled sheet, Kathy was a little ashamed that she had liked being bathed in sweat, smelling a primal sort of sex smell, with Robert's milky fluid trickling out on to her thigh. Gamely she dragged herself out of bed and stood watching him in fascination under the warm stream of water in the shower. She joined him in the shower and was embarrassed to sense his eyes assessing her naked body. She darted a glance at him from under her lowered lashes and blushed.

Robert was sound asleep by the time she came back to bed. He looked so handsome, so virile, and yet so childlike as he slept. He was her husband, her lover, *hers* forevermore. She was so excited by the immensity of that thought that she could not settle down and go to sleep. She looked forward to sleeping naked next to him, their hot flesh pressed together all night long.

But just before she crawled into bed, she saw a spot of red on the sheets. She stared at this bloodstain which had been her hymen, and she sighed. Thank God, she had saved herself for Robert. She had a sudden, sentimental inspiration. In the morning she would take a pair of scissors and snip out that pinkish-red blotch from the sheets. She would save her virginity all her life. She would maybe even mount it in a scrapbook. Again, she sighed.

As she lay sleepless beside Robert in the deepening night, she allowed herself a slow playback of the night's experience. She had liked him touching her everywhere. She had especially liked how earthy and sated and giving it had made her feel when he was inside her. And strong. She had never felt stronger or more powerful than when he had come inside her. There had been such a supreme triumph in having him so close, in finally being not empty but full. She savoured the remembrance of that feeling of power and satiety, of hunger and want finally appeased.

"Robert!" It was the middle of the night, but she shook him until she roused him. "Just think, Robert! We can do this every night for the rest of our lives! Every night! Isn't that wonderful!" Robert's only answer had been to turn groggily away and go back to sleep.

Kathy had been hoping that after she woke him, he would make love to her again. She had imagined he would let go inside her just as the sun came up, so that they would begin the first dawn of their marriage soldered together. Instead, she had to be content to be beside him reveling in her heady dreams.

Robert was wonderful. He was a wonderful man, a wonderful lover, wonderful in every way. She hugged herself tightly. "I'm the luckiest woman on earth," she said softly to herself in a nice warm wallow of blissful fulfillment and heightened sensitivities. "Only twenty years old and already I'm on my way to living happily ever after. Yes, there is some point to being alive!"

The thread of Kathy's charmed reminiscences was rudely cut by the air hostess. There was a crackle of static over the loudspeaker system and finally an announcement in Arabic and then in English.

"Welcome to the Kingdom of Saudi Arabia."

Chapter 11

Delfin Cruz, the Filipino driver the company sent to collect us from Dhahran airport and take us to the company's 'village' in Al-Khobar for a couple of days stop-over rest, peered up into the cloudless cobalt sky through his black lensed sunglasses as he waited for our plane. No sign of it yet.

Our flight was predictably late. When he arrived at Customs in the afternoon, only the shoeshine man had been waiting by the gate. But now a sweaty mass of Saudi men in wrinkled white robes and dusty head scarves stood tightly pressed together against the chain-link fence. He and the Arabs consulted their watches, sighed, shrugged. The Arabs praised Allah and used their head scarves to mop the perspiration off their faces. Almost seven, and still no plane.

Delfin decided to try the airline counter again. He was due to go off duty in an hour or two. He tried to be civil even as he repeated the question he had been asking this insolent clerk all afternoon. When was Flight Twenty-Three due in?

The Arab shrugged, murmured 'inshallah,' yawned, did not even bother to look up from his newspaper. Then grudgingly the clerk passed on the latest word, mostly in English. "Maybe thirty minutes. 'Inshallah,' maybe more."

Delfin almost shuddered. If a Saudi said something could happen in 'maybe more' than thirty minutes, in Western reckoning that could mean an hour or two or three.

For a long while Delfin stood shading his eyes, looking westward into the setting sun for a plane. Finally, he saw it winking silver in the light, growing bigger and coming closer, the waiting relatives shouting and pointing, the plane finally circling wide over the Gulf and landing with squeals and thuds and bounces on the tarmac.

It took an eternity for the Arab workers to roll up the portable stairway, to unlatch the locks and throw open the door. A swarm of excited men surged down the stairway – Saudis in long white robes, Saudis in business suits, other Arabs in cheap cotton shirts and pants. After a pause Delfin saw us poised in the doorway as though unsure whether we wanted to get off there or not. He thought it would surely take us an hour or more to retrieve our luggage and pass through the bureaucratic maze of Immigration and Customs. He sat down on the bench and wiped the sweat off his forehead.

He got to his feet when he heard a howl from the mob outside Customs. He craned his neck to see if the passengers were coming out yet, but then he settled back on his bench when he saw it was simply an argument over who stood where in line. He hoped we weren't' having too bad a time of it inside the terminal. Saudi bureaucrats were notoriously slow and puffed up with their own importance.

At last Delfin heard a sort of moan from the crowd. The passengers were starting to emerge, but still Delfin hung back. Saudi men were the first ones out and joyous knots of kinsman escorted them off to the parking lot. Bewildered Americans and Europeans were greeted by their Arab guides.

Delfin took a deep breath and walked toward the gate, carrying a placard with the names of four doctors on it.

Going through Customs was a teeth-gnashing ordeal as the contents of our luggage were meticulously and often roughly examined and were then stuffed back any old how. One needed to repack afresh to be able to close one's suitcase. A woman in a line next to ours had her Woman's Own magazines seized and pages ripped out of her Reader's Digest magazine for apparently containing pictures of women that showed too much leg or bosom. A couple of men were taken in for questioning for possessing crucifixes or suspect video cassettes.

At long below-his-breath-swearing last, we emerged from the fastness of the terminal and were immediately met by Delfin calling "Dr. Smith! Dr. Jacobs! Dr. O'Neill! Dr. Waveren!" He helped us load our luggage into the company mini-bus and then we got on board and were off to nearby Al-Khobar.

As we got nearer the seacoast we began to perspire profusely as it became uncomfortably sticky because of the high humidity. We arrived at the company 'village' very late into the night. The company had engineering and other construction and trading interests in the kingdom as well as a medical division which had just won the contract to run the military hospital for a couple of years.

Peter, Frank, Paul, and I were each allocated one of the more luxurious senior staff chalets of the company in the 'village' which was really a complex of housing units, sports and recreation centers, a few palm-studded lawns with automatic water sprinklers, and the company's administrative head office in Saudi Arabia. We were so tired by now that all we wanted was to hit the hay and sleep and sleep and sleep.

The next morning, we met up in the senior staff cafeteria for breakfast. There were marooned-liveried waiters on hand to help you indulge yourself to the limit on the bewildering and exotic choice of things to eat. The cuisine was splendid by any standard. We soon understood why the 'village' cafeteria was the focal point of the Rest and Recreation local leave granted to company employees working for the kingdom.

"I wonder how you were allowed in Saudi with a name like Jacobs; sounds Jewish," Frank inquired of Peter.

"It's not really," Peter answered. "It's a fairly common name where I come form in Belgium. I think it merely means the 'Son of James' in your language."

Peter Jacobs was Flemish. He was slenderly built, probably in his late forties or just over fifty, he had a shiny tonsure, and was a heavy cigarette smoker. He had been a specialist gynecologist and obstetrician with a thriving practice in Brussels for close on twenty years but seemed to have quit his practice under a cloud and in troubled circumstances. It appeared he left because of marital difficulties following a brief affair with a close friend of his stronger-willed wife, Johanna. She was a very attractive woman, about eight years younger than Peter and the daughter of a rich industrialist in Antwerp. She had trained as a Physical Education Instructor and was once a champion Alpine skier.

She had been calling the shots more and more since Peter got into serious financial difficulties in an investment that went terribly wrong. The feeling of being patronized by Johanna who had more financial resources than himself was getting to him with increasing and overwhelming force. They had two daughters, Rita and Maria, and a son, Joseph; they were all at university. To add to his chagrin the children seemed to be largely on their mother's side, except the eldest child, Rita, who was still very fond of her 'Papa.' She was a final year medical student at the University of Ghent and had expressed a wish to follow in her father's footsteps and take up obstetrics and gynecology as a specialty.

Frank O'Neill was born in the border town of Dundalk in the Irish Republic but had spent most of his childhood in the Canadian city of Toronto. He came to Ireland to do his medical training at Trinity College Dublin following the death of his mother. His eldest sister Brieda, a schoolteacher, was married to a Canadian middle-ranking civil servant in Toronto and they lived fairly comfortably in a quiet suburb of the city; the couple had put off having children for a few years to get established financially but when they were very eager to have one Brieda found it difficult to conceive.

Frank was small-statured, spirited, and pugnacious – looking like a bantam cock. He walked with an exaggerated swagger apparently dating from his medical school days when he had fractured both his lower legs in a road traffic accident. He and his friend, Patrick O'Reilly, had too much to drink at a late-night party and were driving home on Patrick's motorcycle with Frank in the pillion seat. They were cruising down a quiet country lane in high spirits when they suddenly became award of a car coming towards them at some speed. All Frank can remember was that Patrick had tried to swerve, albeit ineffectually. Frank was swept on to the roof of the car before falling to the ground when the car pulled up sharply; Patrick was killed instantly. Surprisingly, Frank was knocked unconscious only briefly, but he found he was unable to put weight on either leg.

He was still in an elated and cheeky mood when he was wheeled into the Casualty Department of the nearest hospital unaware that his friend had been fatally injured. The severe-looking plump Casualty Sister ordered him to cut out his maudlin cracks and was about to haul him on to his feet when she realized his lower legs were probably broken. She carefully placed him on a stretcher and after his X-rays he was seen to an orthopaedic doctor who admitted him straight to the ward where he gently pulled the legs straight without an anesthetic, and then put on long leg plaster casts. He was in plaster casts for about four months, and when his casts came off, he got his joint movements back fairly quickly because of his high motivation to make up for lost time in his medical studies, since crucial examinations were in the offing.

When Frank had got his primary medical degrees, and had done his pre-registration jobs, he worked at the University College, Dublin, where he decided to take up Anesthetics as a specialty primarily because he thought that would give him a quicker and better chance of getting to the top; the competition for career training posts in the usual first choice specialties like General Medicine, General Surgery, Orthopedics, Obstetrics, and Gynecology was getting increasingly cut-throat and a lot often depended on who backed your application.

Frank had met Rosine Fitzpatrick in Dublin where they were fellow medical students. They had worked together at the University College Dublin where Rosine's father was a Professor of Medicine. They got engaged after two years of wooing by Frank and soon after an engagement party for Rosine's best friend, Mary; Frank had literally swept Rosine off her feet at the party, but Rosine had said 'No' to their making love in an upstairs room until they were engaged.

Since then they had been planning to marry at some suitable time for the past three or four years but had not come round to it yet. And lately Rosine had been indicating that though she was keen to marry Frank she was equally keen on pursuing her medical career as a psychiatrist. She wasn't quite ready to settle down and start a family.

Frank was also having problems from members of the Irish republican Army (IRA) who had been pestering him more recently in his home border town of Dundalk for at least moral support. Then some of them started to demand protection money and he had told them to push off. Well, though he understood their aims and might even support them emotionally, when he heard the rantings of Ian Paisley across the border, he was not going to be an IRA recruit. A few days later he was so disgusted when he had to anaesthetize a young woman who had been brutally shot and 'knee-capped' by the IRA for supposedly being an RUC informer because her sister had married a British solider, that he had decided to get away from it all for a while and come to Saudi Arabia.

Paul van Waveren was born in Bandung, Java, in the Dutch East Indies where his Dutch father had been a well-known dental surgeon until the Japanese invasion during the last war. Then he was taken prisoner and was forced to join a work-gang building railways for the occupying Japanese forces. Paul and his mother had been sent by boat to Paramaribo in Dutch Guiana just before the Japanese overran Java; they arrived safely but some of the boats evacuating Dutch nationals from Java to the Dutch West Indies were sunk with considerable loss of life. Although Paul's father, Jean-Paul, had survived the war and the torture he endured under the Japanese and had returned to Amsterdam following the Japanese surrender, he was a broken man and died of a stroke in bed five years later.

Paul always was fond of memories of his early childhood days in Bandung where he was able to roam and explore surrounding forests often with mixed-blood children of his own age, plus lots to eat and the loving devotion of his parents before they were separated by the war. He had acquired an insatiable desire to travel and explore places, and frequently dreamed about going back to the Far East and to Java in particular.

However, as he grew up, he heard disturbing accounts about the Dutch East Indies that made him feel perhaps the Dutch weren't much loved in their former colonies. He heard accounts of how oppressive the Dutch administration had been initially and about their deliberate policy of mixing-up the races to neutralize and blur their specific identities and aspirations, as well as their ruthless elimination of the elite of the subject races. Later on, maybe a bit late in the day, their colonial policy became more enlightened and caring.

Paul worked for a couple of years in Surinam, the former Dutch Guiana, a few years after qualifying a s a doctor in Amsterdam. Then he was off to the Far East to Indonesian Borneo and Java where he spent a year each in Surabaya and Bandung working as a pediatrician. In Bandung he managed to trace the remains of their old home before the Japanese occupation. It had been used by the local Japanese army commander as his operational headquarters at the time of saturation bombing and massive destruction of Jakarta by the Japanese. Most of the house had been blown up when the Japanese forces began to withdraw from Java.

From Java, Paul went on to South Africa to work in the pediatric unit of a local hospital near Soweto. Here his patients were essentially from the local African population. He was not popular with the Afrikaaner police in the area who suspected him of pro-African National Congress (ANC) and 'Kaffir' sympathies. Paul had met Winnie Mandela, wife of the imprisoned nationalist Nelson Mandela, several times. He put on a brave face when the poor, white Afrikaners taunted him of being a 'Kaffir-Lover,' and told him to go back where he came from.

The increasingly ferocious and cruel oppression of the stubborn young Sowetan blacks by the security forces made Paul shudder.

How tyranny reacted upon the tyrant, he said to himself.

Apart from the Pass Laws, the Group Areas Act and the Race Classification Act would have to be at least adjusted - if not abolished - to avoid the inflammable mixture of circumstances found in Soweto from exploding into an inferno of bloody riots that could engulf the whole country. Paul was convinced that the white South Africans were so hooked on the Good Life that only a decided economic threat which endangered their dream life would waken them to reality. A reality they'd been deliberately shutting their eyes to. How this would come about he wasn't at all sure.

When Paul first arrived in South Africa, he spent a couple of months in Johannesburg. It was there he met and fell in love with a Greek South African, Nana Kaklamanis, whose father had a thriving shipping business. Paul found Nana very supportive when he initially started working in Soweto, and they were soon engaged. But that support didn't last long.

Soon the South African secret police started to lean on her to become an informer. Her attitude to him changed, and she began to sneer at his associations with the native Sowetans. Paul found out that there had been covert threats to Nana's father and the shipping business, so to save her from having to choose between their marriage and her family, Paul broke off their engagement and left South Africa.

He returned to Amsterdam, but soon got bored and restive working in a local hospital, so when he saw the advert for an experienced pediatrician to work in a Saudi Arabian military hospital, he had no second thoughts about leaving.

Chapter 12

The American Project Manager of 'the village,' Mr. Lee Rogers, took Peter, Paul, Frank, and me to the town of Al-Khobar the following day in his air-conditioned Impala for some shopping

It was March. The season of 'Shemal' weather. Howling cold north winds and harsh bitter blinding sandstorms swept through the Saudi deserts from the Iraqi border straight through to Yemen.

We got off at a make-shift car park and at once the street smells assaulted us, the sharp pungent ammonia reek of urine, the odor of human and animal feces, the smoke of burnt meat, the clouds of heavy cooking spices, the whiffs of expensive musky French perfume. We listened, then, to the sounds of modern urban Saudi, the hooting horns, the screech of brakes applied in panic as heavily veiled women walked blindly into the paths of oncoming cars.

We passed these masked women nervously huddled together as the wind billowed their robes out like sheets on a clothesline. They walked single file down a narrow street, close to a wall, the hidden slits of their eyes trained on the sandy ground beneath their bare henna-painted feet. Apparently, it would never do for a Saudi woman to meet the glance of a passing man. It would be even less prudent to walk carelessly through the littered heaps of tin-cans, the rusty nails, broken glass, and the rock-hard mounds of sheep dung. Their black skirts swirled through the urban debris as they picked their way down the street with precisely calculated paces. The wild wind was a constantly sighing wail, and the women fought the wind as they shuffled along.

I soon learnt that no Saudi ever rushes anywhere unless absolute disaster, salacious gossip, or fantastic profits are at stake.

We veered into the labyrinthine lanes of the souk, twisting, and weaving our way through the vegetable and fruit stalls, past the spice men and the gold and silver merchants, alongside the money changers and the sellers of camel saddles and live sheep and truck replacement parts.

By now we were dripping and almost wilting from the sauna-like effect of the high humidity of Khobar town. Soon the muezzins were calling their faithful to prayer and the shop shutters began to come down smartly as the religious police prowled about self-importantly. As people hurriedly emptied the shops and stalls, an elderly American couple bumped against Mr. Rogers. There seemed to have been instant recognition of each other.

"Lee, Honey!" exclaimed the lady. "Fancy meeting you here!"

She was Alma Lawrence. She and her husband Jim had just arrived at the Aramco compound in Dhahran from California on a sentimental trip. They had known Lee Rogers when he was a rascally neighborhood boy in California.

Jim Lawrence had been one of the pioneer geologists that Aramco had sent out to the Middle East when, in 1933, a consortium of American oil companies had paid the king of

Saudi Arabia a down payment of only thirty thousand British pounds to grant them a sixty-year monopoly concession over the eastern half of his country.

When the Saudi King, Abdul Aziz, had signed the pact to allow the 'Nazrani,' infidels - those Christian followers of Jesus of Nazareth - to search the desert for oil, Jim Lawrence had first signed on for the difficult post because he would earn three thousand dollars more a year than he would have in the Texas, California, or Oklahoma oil fields. He needed the extra money so that he and Alma could get married, and so they could save up to buy their own home.

When he returned to the Saudi shore after a preliminary visit, Jim was convinced the biggest jackpot on earth was hidden there. The rich oil fields of America were shallow puddles compared with the deep black viscous seas that lay under the Middle East.

Shortly after the turn of the century the British, then the Russians, and finally the French had begun to drill the petroleum fields of Iran, Iraq, and the Persian Gulf. The Europeans had persuaded backward and impoverished kings and shahs and 'shaykhs' to sign 'concession' agreements for paltry sums in exchange for monopoly mineral rights over entire blocs of countries. Even though the Americans had come late to the Middle East oil bonanza, they had been blessed with a fantastic stroke of buccaneer luck.

Now all Jim wanted was the satisfaction of finding the best fields himself and seeing those wonderfully stinking black geysers spurt into the sky. The Number Two field he thought of as his very own. The way he felt, he wouldn't mind if his fate was to pass all his days in the wild, simple infinities of his desert. He decided where to drill, and then he had insisted they go deeper, long after others had wanted to give up.

He would never forget the day that well came in and commercial quantities of oil first gushed from it. He had just received a letter from Alma which ended '....my heart aches so for the wanting of you, Honey… New Year's resolution for you – write at *least* once a week! Better twice or thrice…. Lots of and lots of love…. A. XXX'

At first Jim's infatuation with the Arabs had been a matter of smells and sounds and sensations, the aroma of cardamom-scented coffee freshly roasted at dawn, the lonesome tinkle of water on hot cracked skin. As time had passed, he had become more and more drawn to the primitive tribal life of the nomadic 'Bedouin.' He had begun to press for assignments that would take him further out into the desert.

Jim had taken to sleeping in a black goat-hair tent. He had ridden the high dunes by camel. He had hunted gazelles with a falcon on his wrist. He had sat silent and motionless in his dusty robes for hours beside flickering campfires. He had begun to experience a wild fierce leaping joy as he flirted with Arab life here in the scorching solitude of this endless desert.

Always, when Jim thought about Saudi oil and the Arabs and himself, he ended up with a mass of contradictions. He loved the oil business, and he loved the primitive life of the Bedouin, but common sense told him the two could not coexist for long.

...

Musa brooded yet again over why Allah had seen fit to make him a guide for the 'Nazrani' who invaded and degraded his world. When King Abdul Aziz had signed the pact that allowed the infidels to search the desert, he had asked the elders of Musa's tribe, the Al-Murrah, to assign one of their own as 'rafiq' protector for the Americans. It was a matter of Musa's personal honour and the collective honour of the Al-Murrah that he safeguard the Americans against all dangers, even at the price of his own life.

Though he had wanted to pass all his days among the black tents of the Al-Murrahs in the deep red dunes of the desert, it must have been written in the great book of life that his destiny was different from his ancestors. The best of the Al-Murrahs had all drawn lots, and Musa had been one of the losers. It had become his fate to shadow the geologist, Jim Lawrence.

Musa's father, Ahmed, like all the Arabs, was younger than he looked, perhaps in his late forties. Before the turn of the century, when Ahmed was in his early teens, he had learned the ways of the Bedouin with another boy who was to grow up to be the King of Arabia, for the tribe of Al-Saud had sent Abdul Aziz to learn desert craft from the noble tribe of Al-Murrah. Later, Ahmed had fought under the standards of his boyhood friend when Abdul Aziz had ridden to victory over most of the Arabian Peninsula.

When after twenty-four years of warfare Abdul Aziz had united virtually all the tribes to form 'Saudi' Arabia, Ahmed could boast that he was the friend of a king. Legend had it that Ahmed and King Abdul Aziz were still allies and comrades. They were two of a kind: proud patriarchs, fierce fighters, shrewd bargainers.

And the Saudis were not just any Arabs, nor any Muslims; they were Wahhabi, members of a strict and puritanical sect who were as different from the masses of freewheeling Muslims as fundamentalist Southern Baptists were from Roman Catholics.

The Wahhabi strain of Islam was the state religion in Saudi. They did not drink alcohol, smoke cigarettes, dance, sing, go to the movies, or otherwise engage in any fun-loving devilry. Religious police flogged men who refused to join the five-times-daily prayers in the mosques.

Criminals were punished according to a harsh medieval code recommended thirteen centuries ago in the Koran. Murders were beheaded, the hand or feet of thieves were severed, adulterous women were stoned to death. In the towns women covered their faces when they ventured from their walled houses, for they lived by a strict code of seclusion.

. . .

Saudi Arabia was one of the most remote and isolated backwaters of the world. But Jim had drawn up the geological maps and run tests on the oil from the Number Two well. Saudi Arabia had so much oil that he was sure that someday it would be one of the richest places on earth.

Yet Jim worried that a sudden influx of great wealth might destroy this brave, simple, ancient way of life. When he had camped with the Arabs, Jim felt he was witnessing the end of a world. He believed the people were romantic and wild and free and more moral than any white men he had ever met. Still, he tried not to be carried away with misplaced romanticism.

Health care, education, new and plentiful water sources, electricity, roads, trucks, telephones, and indoor plumbing would make the lives of these Arabs less difficult. Still, he feared they might lose that was best in them, the inner harmony and integrity of their desert hearts and souls. Sometimes, Jim thought that all he and other Americans were bringing to Saudi was muck and stench and ambiguity and trouble. When he tried to come to rational conclusions about Saudi's future, he always ended up feeling uneasy and ambivalent. But still Jim hated to expel himself from this arid Eden. Before this culture vanished forever, he wanted to understand and experience all Saudi had to offer.

Jim often squandered many an hour haggling in dirty tents with dusky Al-Murrah tribesmen whenever new fields were being drilled for oil. He had been in Saudi long enough to know that negotiations would not even begin in earnest until he and Musa's male kinsmen and the interpreter had drunk their tiny ritual cups of fruity Arab coffee and then their large ritual glasses of sweet Arab tea. Jim's knees would ache and his buttocks get numb as he politely sat with his heels tucked under him on the itchy camel hair blanket. He was no stranger to the sluggish rhythm of Bedouin life. He would often rock on his haunches to try to shake some circulation back into his legs. Slyly, he would angle his wrist so he could see the face of his watch.

Usually, a boy stoked wood on the fire, and another expertly, with great ceremony, poured a mix of waters from three different jugs, representing three different desert wells, into a tarnished brass beaker. One boy would reach into a sack to take a handful of pea-green coffee pods and begin grilling them in a skillet. When the beans had sizzled to an aromatic beige, a boy scooped d them into a brass mortar and pounded them until the camp rang with a sound like Sunday church bells.

They would then collect a handful of tiny grey seeds and return to the fire and pound these seeds until the cardamom and the coffee were a uniform grey dust. They added the spiced coffee to the boiling water and carefully set the beaker on and took it off the fire until the contents had boiled three times. Then they strained what remained with a length of date palm, tasted a few drops themselves, and nodded in satisfaction as they picked up a stack of thimble-size cups in their other hand. They would smile at Jim and offer him the first and most honoured cup of the viscous orangish swirling liquid dynamite.

Jim would give them a gracious guest-to-host smile and take an exquisitely small swallow of the tiny cup of bitter brew. In his years of making desert camp with Musa, he had learned not only how much of this peppery, clovelike coffee he should drink to be polite but also how much he could drink without coming down with diarrhea. Fewer than three cups wasn't very polite, but more than four wasn't healthy.

Jim often wondered at how small the Al-Murrah human settlement were compared with the vastness of the desert, and at the fragility of man's hold on life here. Dangers and menace were everywhere. There were snakes and lethal scorpions in the desert and sharks and eels in the sea. There was early death from oasis 'harara,' or fever, and cholera and malaria and a host of other sicknesses that never struck back in California.

There were the daily torments of the heat and humidity, the packs of big brown rats, and the swarms of stinging black flies and dive-bombing, kamikaze locusts.

When they came, you felt suicidal. They thumped and landed everywhere. These most hateful creatures, staring at you with their beady old-men's eyes while they cling with hard serrated legs. In a bad year you emerged in the morning into a pelting storm of the insects. They would take wing like small aircraft as you approached, and their rustling was a big forest in the storm, their settling on a roof like the beating of tropical rain. Then the ground became invisible in a sleek brown surging tide – it was like being drowned in locusts, submerged by the loathsome, glistening flood.

The intensity of the blinding spotlight that was the sun could easily force one's eyes to settle into a permanent wrinkly squint. And at noon the implacable baking sun, the heat, the heavy damp air was usually too much. Nothing at all would move in the air except too many waves of heat; heat so overheavy it seemed to transform stationary objects – a tent, a palm tree, a broken-down Toyota tuck – into wavering shimmerings of mirage.

And always there were the filth and the backwardness and the suspicion of hostile Arabs who wanted the infidel Americans to stop looking for oil and go away and leave them to their medieval squalor.

But again, one easily fell in love with the primal romance of the Saudi desert at sunrise and sunset, its silent infinities, and the way the light caught the sand and bathed it in glowing hues. As you looked at the horizon where the sun was setting you were stunned by the fireworks and the flickers of purple and indigo and mauve and blood red.

The blue-black darkness of the Saudi night would fall suddenly like a veil. If you lay on your back in the desert the stars and the moon were always so bright that, you could stretch your hands up to the sky and pretend the heavens were within grasp. Looking out at the Saudi desert you could too easily lose yourself in the towering, womanly undulations of the dunes. Something about the vastness of the desert and the smallness of man makes God as inescapable as grains of sand here. No wonder the Middle Eastern deserts had spawned so many religions. Mystics and prophets and saints had repeatedly heard the terrible and wonderful insistent thundering voice of God in these deserts.

Chapter 13

Jim and Alma had come to visit, probably for the last time, the foreign school in Bahrain they had helped to found in memory of their son, Henry. He had been born at the American hospital on Dhahran by caesarian section following a difficult labour, and when Alma was carrying him in the early months of her pregnancy, she was sick all the time, and frightened, and as fretful as a baby.

Alma, Jim reflected then, was as fragile as a fern, and a fern could not survive this withering life in the desert. Mostly he regretted bringing her to Saudi, even though she had hounded him to let her come, even though he doubted he could last long in Saudi without her. They had been in love, it seemed sometimes, for all their lives. They had started as childhood sweethearts back in California, and later, when he was away at college, she had written him at least a letter a day.

Henry had drowned tragically in the Gulf, aged four, when the engine of a Bahrain bound launch that had cast off for a recreational sea cruise suddenly coughed and died. This was followed by black smoke rising in a cloud from the engine room.

Henry screamed as a sudden blue flash from the engine room was brighter for an instant than the sun. Alma had shuddered when a louder clap like thunder echoed over the water.

As Jim, Alma, and Henry huddled close together, an explosion rent the air. Smoke belched over the deck and there was a whoosh of hot air. They were thrown off their feet. A deafening boom sounded, white light crackled and in an instant they were sprawled back in a tangled heap on the deck. There were agonized screams from the far side of the deck, frenzied shrieks in Arabic and English. The deck pitched very violently back and forth. When Jim and Alma came to, more or less, they realized that Henry was missing and had been blown overboard into that shark-and barracuda-infested sea.

Alma had known that sharks lurked just under the surface of the Gulf waters. She was thankful that in her few years in Saudi she had not yet spotted one. However, Jim had told her that barracudas were in fact the deadliest fish in the sea. Worse than sharks. A helluva lot of swimmers who had been reported killed by sharks were really done in by barracuda. Jim had shaken his head and continued:

"Barracuda have razor teeth, and they'll go after anything that moves. They've been known to rip a man to pieces, even very close to shore."

"Ripped to pieces?" Alma had shivered, edging closer to her husband. She burst into tears. "Jim," she sobbed, "I'm afraid here. So afraid."

Now the full grisly horror of what could have happened to Henry gripped her. "Henry! Henry!" Alma screamed disconsolately as she clung desperately to Jim.

Faint human cries drifted on the wind; bits of wreckage sailed through the air, splashed, sank. Jim and Alma found themselves in the sapphire blue waters of the Persian Gulf clinging to the listing side of a make-shift raft. How they got ashore they could not really remember, but drifting near them among bits and pieces of wreckage from the boat was Henry's favourite red and blue baseball hat which he had been wearing for the outing.

Alma was lying next to Jim on the double bed in their 'honoured-guest' Aramco air-conditioned bungalow in Dhahran, looking at the sepia-toned photograph of her Henry taken a day before the fatal trip to Bahrain. She'd persuaded Jim to make this final trip to the Middle East to help finally exorcise the demon of the deep dark swirling memories of Henry's death in those killing waters of the Gulf.

She remembered, as if it were yesterday, when she had first gone to Saudi as a bride. She had been so young, so innocent, so bedazzled by bright and shining illusions. She, Alma, sometimes could hardly remember how it had felt to be that young and credulous. She had been the world's greatest champion of romance. She had fervently believed every fairy tale she had ever heard about Prince Charming and white horses and Arabian nights and living happily ever after.

But only later had she learned that romance, like all the other quicksilver thrills in her life, was not always what it appeared to be. She remembered how she had fallen so absolutely in love with Jim that nothing on earth or in heaven – nothing! – could ever have kept her from being with him. She had blissfully gone off with him to the magical medieval kingdom between the seas.

Saudi – how she loved and hated it. To her Saudi was all black and white, a hot place on eternal emotional fire, gentle and brutal, pure and corrupted, gorgeous and squalid. Very few people in America understood what she said about the white light and the dark shadows that were Saudi. Either people there thought Saudi was one big playground for super-rich playboy princes or they thought it was all dunes and derricks and wild-eyed religious fanatics. The Saudi she knew was so much more complex - so much better and yet so much worse - than the myths and the lies that shrouded it.

Saudi was the country everyone loved to hate. The West hated Saudi for quadrupling the price of oil triggering the panic of the energy crisis and fueling in international financial recession. Even other Arabs were jealous of Saudi for its money, despised Saudi for its arrogance, and ridiculed Saudi for its ignorance. S.A.U.D.I. was said to stand for Savage... Arrogant... Uncouth... Dirty... and Ignorant...

What we should do with those filthy Saudis, Americans sometimes told her after they had a few drinks, was either bomb the place off the map and 'nuke the Gulf' or land the Marines and take back 'our' oil fields.

Alma soon recalled the course, heavy black fabric of the 'abba,' the cloak women in Saudi wore over all their other clothes. And then the 'burqa,' the mask, and remembered her shock the first time she had seen one. Why, she wondered, did everyone rant on so about veils when it was the masks women wore along the Gulf that were really the atrocity.

The mask was a face-size slab of dense fabric, of sewn-together layers of opaque, cheap rayon and taffeta and polyester, with two slits only as wide as button-holes for the eyes, a slight fullness to make room for the bridge of the nose, and three ties at the back to hold it in place. She learned that the Arab women had to breathe with the mask on, in quick, nearly breathless shallow pants through flared nostrils and parted lips.

Alma had been embarrassed to admit to Jim that since she had come to Saudi, just as soon as the oil company had allowed wives to come, she had found herself more and more often bereft of sound commonsense reasons for everything and anything. Most of the time she blamed her odd new moods, her disquieting new tendencies toward superstition on nothing more significant than the awful, damp, disabling heat. None of them were at their best in that heat. It was the maddening heat that had made her do as their Arab houseboy suggested. She had out a blue stone charm in Henry's crib to ward off the Evil Eye.

She often felt an itchy prickly-heat rash budding on her chest and at the back of her neck and where her thighs rubbed together when she walked. She frequently felt sweat beading her forehead, in her armpits, under her breasts. Often as she lifted her arm to blot the perspiration off her forehead with the sleeve of her dress, she got a whiff of herself. When she worked up a sweat out in the sand patch she called a garden, the wet smell of work was sweet and decayed. When she made love with Jim on their gummy cotton sheets, the hot smell of sex was yeasty. When she sat too long waiting in the sun, the steamy smell of impatience was thick and stagnant.

But the strongest, gamiest smell of all, the smell that would not be masked by cornstarch or deodorant or cheap jasmine cologne, was the rank animal smell of her own fear. She tried always to laugh off her misgivings. The worse she felt, always, the more she laughed. She had been acting positively giddy ever since she had come to Saudi. From the shimmering sapphire sea of the Gulf to the relentless orange sun above, and to the gritty white sand beneath her, dangers and menace were everywhere.

She could recite a litany of fervent curses upon 'this cursed land.' Yet it had not always been so. When she, Alma, had been fresh to Saudi, she had written rapturous letters home about its virgin beauty. Once, the exotic landscape had seemed to her paradisical. Once the Arabs had seemed to her wise and serene and larger than life.

But Alma had exhausted all her romantic delusions about Saudi. She soon wanted out. She was ashamed she did not have the stamina to stick it out in Saudi. She would have liked to have been an altogether heroic pioneer woman who thrived on hardship. But she was only Alma Crosby Lawrence, a sheltered, fragile, and very homesick twenty-two-year-old American girl.

Chapter 14

It seemed to Jim that he always ended up creating a furor whenever he came back to Dhahran from an oil-exploration camp. On this trip he had raised hell with the company team from San Francisco about America's support of the newly born state of Israel.

Saudi Arabia had sent a token force of Bedouin to fight as soon as the Zionist state was proclaimed in May 1948. And after the United States rushed to recognize and support Israel, some Arabs had vowed revenge by disrupting America's oil supplies. A couple of days ago Jim had pounded on his supervisor's desk and asked why the oil companies weren't lobbying in Washington for a saner American foreign policy.

"I know the Arabs," he said. "I camp with them, talk with them, understand them. Palestine to the Arabs is a gut emotional issue, and someday they will make America pay dearly for coming down on the side of the Jews."

But the men from San Francisco had taken Jim aside and whispered secrets in his ear. The oil industry would continue to do all it could to hold the line against American support of

Israel. But in the meantime, the United States' ambassador in Jeddah had been assured by the royal family that that whatever happened in Palestine would not affect the American oil concession. Moreover, Saudi Arabia had sabotaged an Arab League effort to shut down American oil production. Saudi Arabia would never turn against America. Jim's boss had patted the back pocket of his trousers: "Saudi Arabia," he said, "is right here!"

Jim looked up to the peak of Jebel Dhahran, where in the uncertain dawn light, the gas flare burn-offs smoked up the pure desert air. He sniffed the wind like an Arab's sleek saluki dog and nearly gagged as he took in a nose full of the rotten-egg smell wafting over from the nearby oil-stabilizing plant. "This place stinks," Jim said with finality.

His fellow Americans thought him most eccentric because he preferred to camp alone in the desert or off with the Arabs rather than live in the air-conditioned bungalow to which he was entitled. He was tolerated only for his knack for finding oil. Perversely, just to increase his own misery, Jim sniffed in the fetid air again. Arabs said the sulpher stench was sweet compared with the other corruptions the oil industry had brought to a Saudi that had been altogether innocent not so very long ago. The Saudis looked the other way and tolerated Americans drinking liquor within the boundaries of the Eastern Province, and alcoholism had become an epidemic among the bored, homesick expatriates. Roughnecks held nightly gambling sessions in bunkhouses.

A certain type of fugitive man who was running away from a nagging wife or a ruined life had begun to turn up in Saudi, some that Dhahran was becoming the American oilman's French Foreign Legion. Jim's Arab friends were worried that their country was being corrupted from within by the presence of all these exceptions to their rules.

Jim looked out beyond the high steel fence toward the desert. There were shadowy piles of sand and bulldozers and half-finished constructions littering the oil-company compound at Dhahran. He shook his head. He did not know much about the sociological stresses and strains of rapid change. But he was a geologist, and he knew about oil. In the report he had just presented, he had estimated that more than half the world's oil reserves lay under this bleakly beautiful Middle Eastern terrain.

He scanned the flat horizon to the east, toward the nearby Gulf coast, where thousands were working overtime to shuttle oil from the bottomless wells of Saudi to the insatiable factories of the West. Postwar rebuilding and retrenching and expansion had created an unquenchable thirst for oil. Even the United States, which until now had always exported its own excess oil, had begun to import it this year. High quality crude was far cheaper to extract here than anywhere else in the world. A barrel of oil that cost sixteen cents to produce in Saudi cost one dollar and seventy-three cents to produce in Texas.

Moreover, the long-term oil-concession agreements signed by the Saudi king nearly twenty years ago meant that Americans had an uncontested monopoly to find and develop and market these oceans of cheap and choice oil Petroleum profits were higher and risks lower in the Mideast than anywhere else in the world, and a massive Saudi oil rush was the result.

During the Second World War, when it hadn't been possible to ship much oil over treacherous seas, production had been, at most, fifteen thousand barrels a day. But by the end of next year, 1954, it was expected to be a staggering half million barrels a day. That boom would not have been possible without an extraordinary expansion of pumping, pipeline, and treating facilities. Even before the war had ended, a pipeline had been laid under the sea to Bahrain and a huge oil refinery had been built along the Saudi cost.

Ras Tanura had been transformed into a deep-water tanker port through the construction of a seven-mile causeway and trestle fingering out into the Gulf. Aramco had begun building a massive 'Tapline' pipeline across a thousand miles of scorching desert from the Persian Gulf of Saudi to the Mediterranean coast of Lebanon. Along the way, too, three entirely new towns had been built as well as an international airport, two hundred miles of road, and a railroad linking Dhahran to the Saudi capital city of Riyadh. Jim knew Aramco was planning to double its production in five years, and he wouldn't be surprised if it increased tenfold before it was all over.

Jim felt better after wrapping a flowing red checkered cotton head scarf that was called a 'ghutra' around his head and held it in place with a black 'igal' cord. He and the other pioneer American oilmen had begun wearing Arab headgear years ago because of the fierceness of the desert sun. He was about to leave again for an oil exploration camp. He ground the gears of his Kenworth truck, painted like all the hundreds of Aramco vehicles, a vivid and perhaps lifesaving red which an airplane could spot in even the most remote stretches.

He passed through the gate and struck out on the new Aramco desert road. Every five weeks he had come in from his wildcat oil-exploration camp to file progress reports. And by the time he finally finished his prep work and his meeting and let the alleged refinements of Dhahran behind him, he breathed an audible sigh of relief. Especially now that Alma was back in California he felt suffocated inside those temperature controlled shacks they shipped in from America.

"Thank God that's over," Jim said more to himself more than to Musa beside him.

"El-Hamdulillah" – Allah be praised – Musa echoed in Arabic. He too was glad to be returning to the desert he loved.

Jim concentrated on making good time on the smooth asphalt that stretched forty barren miles southwest to the high dunes of Abqaiq. It was midmorning and time for a break when they arrived at the frontier town. He looked out proudly to where he had brought in the first whopper Abqaiq well eight years ago. He had been first to suspect that a rich dome of oil lay under the desert, not only here, but farther southwest where he had just recently spudded in those new Ain Dar wells. He had a hunch that the oil nearly one hundred and sixty miles southwest at Haradh was part of the same geological structure that lay under Ain Dar.

Back in Dhahran he had just made his case to sink a necklace of new wells between Ain Dar and Haradh, but the cost-conscious Aramco executives had at least for now vetoed his ambitious scheme. Yet Jim thought the largest accumulation of oil ever found anywhere in the world might lie under the desert forty miles from here. Jim downed two small cups of coffee prepared by Musa. Their destination lay at the end of an uncertain desert track slicked down and blackened only by a coating of oil, and they would have to cross this in the killing heat of the day.

Again, they swung out into the desert, but this time Jim was in a ripping good mood. He loved the challenge of this tough dangerous black ribbon through grey wilderness. He came close to contentment only when he was pitting himself against fate in the arid desert.

In the past few years, as oil production had increased, Aramco had learned to jump every time, a Saudi prince snapped his fingers. The oil company had branched out into social and economic development, sending Saudis abroad to schools, building roads, and setting up clinics.

Chapter 15

Even after all these years, Jim was impatient at the roundabout slowness of every facet of Arab life. He had yawned as he wished they would get on with it – the tribal ritual of Musa getting married to his cousin Halima, ('the polite.')

In the flickering light of the desert campfire, it seemed that savage ghosts of the fabled tribal past, the spirits of the Islamic warriors who had once swept out from Arabia to secure much of the world for Allah, were alive and unappeased and dancing. It seemed that the decadent ghosts of the opulent future, the only spirits unleashed by the subterranean steel drills, were on their feet and rehearsing complicated new steps and dancing. It seemed that the ambivalent ghosts of the uncertain present, the ambiguous spirits of a world neither here nor there, were dazed and unsure and dancing.

The long, silent, wraithlike line of white-robed, white-scarfed, brown-skinned men, linked at the shoulders with arms intertwined, wavered then seemed to sigh and sway one step closer to the black goat-hair tents. For this dance there was no music of flutes, horns, lutes; only the primitive percussion of a donkey skin drum that pounded slowly, steadily, tiredly, like the heartbeat of an old man. To that somber beat the long line of Al-Murrah tribesmen shuffled their bare feet in the sand, back and forth left to right, a monotonous lead-footed dance.

At the end of the line, suddenly, there was a clatter of steel and a flash of light as a man brandished a sword at the crescent moon. Heads turned, teeth flashed, shoulders straightened, until the sword was once more sheathed and the brotherly line was once again unbroken. From time to time, then, at irregular intervals, the hops and shuffles and swordplay of the men were punctuated by eerie, high-pitched and tongue-warbling screeches of unseen women, the wives and daughters and sisters and nieces and cousins who were assembled in the cloistered privacy of a big black tent.

When the women were quiet, the wind, howling in from the bleak wastes of the open desert, filled the void. Then a camel would groan, a child would cry out, a man would wave a carbine, then shoot it at the sky. The drum would beat on as these men continued their ghostly shuffle.

In the dark shadows just beyond the arc of firelight sat one man who was not of the tribe or spirit of the dancing ghosts. Silent and unmoving he sat through this night, as he had done the night before. To most outsiders the sights and sounds of this mournful midnight desert dance would seem the mythic essence of grief and dread. But Jim Lawrence knew better. He knew that the Al-Murrah were not grieving but celebrating.

Jim searched the shadowy faces for Musa, dancing at his own wedding. Long ago, to strengthen his family ties by taking his cousin as wife, it had been decided that Musa should marry his cousin Halima, who was the daughter of Ahmed's dead older brother. Jim's thoughts trailed a world away, back to California, where courtships were a matter of love and passion instead of family arrangements.

Yesterday he had accompanied Ahmed, Musa, and a pack of other male relatives into Hofuf to get the Imam's religious seal on Musa's marriage contract. Musa had pledged to protect and support Halima who had not witnessed Musa making this vow. But all the kinsmen had watched Musa pay five thousand riyals – about twelve hundred dollars – to set up a proper household for his bride. Ahmed had firmly refused Jim's offer to pay Musa's bride price but had graciously allowed him to give this wedding feast. For Musa had once saved Jim's life when their truck had overturned, and Jim had been trapped under the truck as it caught fire in the desert dunes near Ain Dar.

Since the Al-Murrah were strict Wahhabi fundamentalists, there would be no liquor, music, tobacco, or any dancing except for that ceremonial sword dance of the men. Nor would there be any barefaced contact between Al-Murrah men and women. While the men celebrated here, the women held their own party inside a nearby tent.

The high point of this marriage so far had come when the hundred or so guests feasted on twenty roasted sheep. Jim would have liked to throw a Western-style wedding that all the tribes would have talked about for generations. But he reminded himself that his own yearning for a tiered wedding cake and champagne and rice thrown into the air was of another world.

Suddenly as the drumbeat stopped and Ahmed stepped forward from the line of dancing men, Jim snapped to attention. After two days of ritualized anticipation, the marriage was about to be consummated. Musa would deflower his bride behind the closed flaps of his wedding tent, while every man, woman, and child of this branch of the Al-Murrah sat listening for any sounds of fighting or laughing or gasping in surprise or pleasure. Musa could take ten minutes or ten hours, but eventually blood-stained bits of cloth would have to wave outside the tent as proud proof of the virtue of the bride. As Jim tried to catch the eyes of Musa, he thanked God he hadn't had to do it to Alma the first time with his mother in a ringside seat listening to the sound of their loving.

He watched Musa trading boastful jests with his cousins as he swaggered towards his wife's tent. Then he threw back his shoulders and held up his head and trod softly to the black tent where his bride waited.

How strange, Jim thought, that in a country as puritanical as Saudi a couple's first sexual encounter was so public. And how odd that a husband's first introduction to his wife was the ultimate in intimacy. Yet Jim supposed that what was about to happen behind the closed tent flap was only an old and universal story. Like every other human being in the history of the world, Musa would just have to do his best with as much grace as he could muster, as he blundered through his sexual initiation.

Jim's lips turned up in a smile as he remembered another boy and girl on another night, skin against skin, under white sheets and a calico quilt. He wished some of the magic he had made long ago in a hotel in San Francisco with Alma would rub off tonight on his friend, Musa.

Musa blinked in the sudden dimness. Before him stood a bundle of black cloth that seemed like every other shapeless sack that was a Saudi woman. Musa reminded himself that he had to have sexual relations with whatever sort of creature that was hidden under those homespun folds. His grandfather, his father, his mother, his aunts, his cousins, and Jim Lawrence were sitting outside the tent waiting to hear him take this woman. His virility was at stake. If he took her very fast, maybe they would even make a legend in the tribe about how manly he was.

However, never having been alone with a sexually available woman, Musa was at a loss as how to approach his bride. He stalled for time and prayed for courage, beseeching Allah's blessings and help on what should be the next step in the courtship of his bride. He beckoned to her. "Halima!" From under the black mask and cloak and veil there was muffled noise that did not sound like assent.

"Halima!" His curiosity quickened. "Wife, show me your face!" Musa took a resolute step closer to his wife. But again, she fled from him. She ran from one end of the tent to the other, like a bird beating its wings against the bars of a cage.

Watching the frenzy of her flight, Musa finally remembered the custom. Any Saudi bride with an ounce of virtue – and Saudi women measured their virtue not by the ounce but by the pound – was supposed to engage in hand-to-hand combat before she would even show him her face. Musa leaned against a tent pole and yawned at the prospect of wrestling mask and veil off his cousin.

Musa edged closer to Halima, seized the dangling edge of her black cloak, and whisked it off her.

"La." – No. Again, Halima lunged away from him.

He beseeched Allah again for help, saying pious prayers toward Mecca. A change of tactics would perhaps answer this time.

He sat cross-legged at some distance, and from his pockets brought out and plied her with a series of small presents had had been reserving for when they had consummated their marriage though these presents were not required of him in the marriage contract. First two tinkling silver ankle bracelets someone had bought for him in Cairo, and her delighted laugh at being given these trinkets encouraged Musa in his new tack. He said her laugh tinkled like silver, Now, when he gave her the 'melabas' candy he had bought for her in Hofuf, he laughed and called her 'y'assal,' a woman as sweet as honey. He gave her a fistful of ribbons that he said were green like sweet grass and blue like the sea and yellow like the sun. He gave her a bolt of red cloth – red, he said, like a woman's lips – so that she could make herself a new dress.

Halima laughed again and thanked him gravely for all those thoughtful presents. But when he brought out some choice dates and pomegranates and invited her to share them with him, Halima blushed with dismay. She could not eat these without removing her heavy black cloak and veil and mask. Yet the demands of courtesy and hospitality required that she did. Gallantly Musa offered to turn his back while she ate her share.

"La!" Oh no. She would not be tricked into unveiling herself without a fight. Musa laughed at the failure of his ply, and then he made another proposition. He was willing, he said, to respect his wife's virtue. He would shut his eyes, and after she removed her veil and mask, *he* would put them on while she ate her pomegranates and dates.

She laughed again at the incongruity of a man wearing a woman's mask. For a moment, she forgot her fear of him and what they were supposed to do together in his tent. It was not so long ago, after all, that she and Musa had been children together, playing around the campfires and swimming together in the deep lake-like desert wells.

Everyone said Musa was a good man, a generous man, a brave man, a true son of the Al-Murrah. She was flattered to be her cousin's wife. She knew, however, that she was supposed to make him chase her around the tent and that by now she should be crying out and moaning and protesting loudly enough to wake the spirits of the dead. Instead, she longed to cover Musa's handsome face with kisses.

Musa brought her indecision to an end by leaning over and very gently tugging at her cloak and veil. Halima held her breath as her cocoon slipped down around her shoulders and she felt his fingers touch her hair.

"Soft as the Dahana sands," Musa whispered.

She laughed and did not back away when his fingers fumbled at the ties for a long while, and then seemed to give up. As his fingers stroked the hair of her temples, he whispered to her that she would have to help him remove that mask.

Should she be coy or bold? The tips of his fingers trailed from her hair to her shoulders. The touch of his skin on hers thrilled her. For long tantalizing years she had yearned for the magic hour when this man would finally touch her. In the hot languor of desert afternoons, lying in the heat of the shade, she had imagined his hand in her hair and on her breasts and between her legs. She had waited in agony of sexual lassitude for Musa to make her his. And so, it was too hard to debate any longer whether to untie her mask. It was possible now only to let herself feel the touch of his fingers.

She sat trembling like a gazelle scenting on the wind the dangerous excitement of a predator. His fingers strayed from her shoulders to where the mounds of her breasts should be. Swiftly he drew the black cloak off her shoulders and Halima sighed. As he eagerly touched his fingertips to her breasts, to her waist, back to her breasts again, Halima could feel her blood beginning to pound.

Just as Musa was wondering how he would ever undo her skintight purple robe, to his astonishment this girl who could not even show him her face rose majestically to her feet and threw off her robe. He gasped and his penis went hard as he gazed at her curves and swells and softness.

"Heavens! How beautiful!"

He stumbled to his feet and placed his sweaty hands on her cool, full, high breasts. As he touched them, the tips hardened as if by magic. "So beautiful!" Halima arched her back so that her breasts pointed even higher.

Tenderly, tentatively, he reached out his hands and cupped her breasts. This time his touch made her shudder. Quickly she bent over and slipped off her pantaloons. Carefully she spread them on the blanket and lowered herself so that the white cotton was under her thighs. When she was flat on her back, she giggled, spread her legs, and waited.

Musa took a deep breath. She was the most luscious and hot and willing woman in the world, and she was his. Musa stepped out of his shorts and knelt beside her and resisted his eager impulse to plunge right inside her. This Halima, with the smooth skin and ripe body, was his cousin. If he pushed himself into this girl laid so invitingly before him, he might frighten or hurt her. Yet he was perplexed. If he wasn't going to enter her just yet, what else could he do? He had expected it would be more complicated and that it would take far longer to get where they were now. He supposed they should be talking more. Surely there were words that should be said? But what words? And who should say them?

Halima lay panting. She evidently did not share his desire to talk. Musa was afraid she might laugh if he suggested they pray before the final consummation. Instead, he simply looked at the wonder of her lying open to him. When she panted like this, loudly, so that she would most assuredly be overheard outside, her breasts heaved. He reached out his hand and stroked the satin skin of her breasts which would someday nurse their children.

Halima waited with bated breath as he stroked her slowly, from her breasts to her belly, and then she sighed when finally, he buried his hesitant fingers in the dampness between her legs. She was panting in earnest now, as he touched her for long minutes, but then she was impatient for the ultimate. She peered at Musa from behind her mask.

"I have done something wrong?" Her husky voice was so soft he could hardly hear her. "I do not please you?"

Musa blushed and shook his head and wished he dared to kiss every curve of her silky body. He could heel himself getting harder. He was embarrassed enough to try and hide his reception from her; but this young cousin of his, a girl so modest she still couldn't take off her mask, reached for his penis. He squirmed away from her. He thought it was just another idle tribal boast that Al-Murrah women were so hot-blooded. When she laughed at his modesty, Musa grew even more confused. Did she think they were two camels or two sheep about to mate in a pasture?

But then Halima laughed more gently. "Husband, husband, they are listening outside. I think it is time, husband, to give them something to listen to!"

Musa nervously wet his lips. "You are ready? Now you are ready?"

She nodded her head so definitely her dangling earrings made music. Again he stalled for time. "You are certain?"

She spread her legs even wider.

Musa leaned over his bride even more shyly than before. Gently he fingered her soft breasts, and he let his hands trail down to her rounded belly. As he wandered inevitably lower, she shuddered. Tensely he stared at the mysterious pouting hairless cleft between her legs. When he was a boy, he and once spread a female sheep's hind legs to study the difference between male and female. He conquered his impulse to bend over Halima as he had bent over that sheep, examining her fascinating differences.

He concentrated instead on the possibility of a great shame. He did not know where exactly he should put himself, how to do it and not hurt her. He had been too proud to ask any of the other men. "Allah!" Musa couldn't help praying, out loud, for God's blessed guidance. He would be everlastingly ashamed if he did all this wrong.

"I am waiting!" Halima laughed up at him, "I'll be an old woman before you take me, M-u-s-a…!" She intoned his name, 'Musa,' in a most sensual, deliciously seductive, come-hither voice.

Musa could not postpone it any longer. Even as he knelt between her legs and very slowly lowered himself almost on top of her, Musa continued to fret whether he was doing it right. When the tip of him touched the skin of her thigh, he cried out, for he had swelled so much he feared he would explode out of his own skin. Blindly he thrust it toward her.

Here? Anxiously he pushed against her skin. *Do I put it here?*

"Musa!" In between theatrical pants she called out his name so that everyone outside could hear. "Musa!"

He was encouraged to grope around until he found a kind of warm, moist indentation in her.

He broke into a sweat. Please, Allah, he prayed to himself, guide me, so I don't put it in the wrong place, so I don't hurt my little cousin. Very slowly, very lightly, he pushed himself in just a fraction.

"Allah strengthen thee!" Halima managed to gasp in encouragement as she arched up her hips to receive him "Allah!"

In triumph then he let himself go and pushed harder and deeper. But he could only go so far. He felt her give a little under him. He pressed still harder, still deeper, and then finally he broke though, he was altogether in and was indescribably overwhelmed by the moist, smooth, white-hot feel as he moved inside her. And then, just when he thought the ordeal was over, he felt Halima moving under him, together with him; he felt her arms close around him. This was wonderful, wonderful…

"Allah!" He called out his pleasure for God to witness. He had never felt this good in all his life. He pushed harder, deeper, faster. "Halima! My Halima!" They shook together in delight on the blanket in the sand.

From outside the tent then, after the two of them finally were quiet, they could hear the women's 'zaghareit' joy-cries. The women had been listening to the progressive sounds of their intimacies so closely that they knew precisely when to cheer.

Musa lifted his head from Halima's breast and looked in astonishment at his bride. He had been so obsessed with her body that he had forgotten her face. After what they had just shared, how could it be that she was still wearing her mask? Masterfully he seized the bottom of the mask and ripped it off. For the first time he beheld the softly laughing brown face of his beautiful Halima. Her melting saucer-like eyes black and glistening. Her mouth was red and laughing. Shyly she giggled up at him. She was more embarrassed that he was seeing her face than she had been to let him take her body.

Timidly, then, she pointed from the gifts of ankle bracelets to the blood stains on her pantaloons.

"My gift to you," she said in a very small voice.

He hugged her, then kissed her on her red full lips. Their arms were round each other as they held each other close for long minutes.

"El-Hamdulillah!" – Praise be to God – Musa heard himself say as he very gently let go of Halima.

Chapter 16

Jim Lawrence had used his influence to secure for Faisal, a cousin of Musa, an Aramco graduate scholarship to study petroleum engineering in Texas. First, he had attended the foreign school in Bahrain that Jim helped to found in memory of his son, Henry. Then, before coming to Texas, Faisal had been to the American University of Beirut where he studied Engineering and Economics.

When he finished his training, he was not going to be interested in any desk job in the oil business; he wanted to be 'a very big boss.' He had very fond memories of the American University of Beirut. 'Very beautiful. Gardens. Many trees. From the campus we looked out over the Mediterranean.'

One of the first things that struck Faisal on arrival in America was the incomprehensible obsession with race. In Texas, dark skin was anathema when he came there in the summer of 1956. There were signs, however, that perhaps the day was dawning when all this would change. The US Supreme Court had ruled two years ago that the segregation of American schools must end – and even though last winter an ugly mob at the University of Alabama had all but stoned a young Negro girl – still that formerly all-white campus had begun to desegregate.

And after an old black seamstress, Rosa Parks, was arrested last winter for refusing to move to the back of a Montgomery bus, a coalition of Negro ministers led by the Reverend Martin Luther King, Jr, – a bland young man with solemn good looks – had begun a successful boycott of that city's buses. At the start of the boycott, Reverend King had addressed a congregation at the local Mount Zion church and the place was jammed to the doors by people. His rhetoric then was a bit heady but his iron refusal to meet violence with violence helped to encourage more tolerance and understanding in the public and to make the United States a more colour-blind society.

But that did not happen overnight. The Ku Klux Klan still burned crosses across the South, and white citizen's councils ruled below the Mason-Dixon line, and everyone 'coloured' had to use separate restaurants and public toilets and drinking fountains. And it did not take too long before the Reverend Dr. Martin Luther King Jr., himself, was fatally wounded by an assassin's bullet.

Faisal reflected that at home in Saudi skin varied from white to black, just as it did here in Texas, and for the same reason. Black-skinned and brown-skinned Africans had been imported to Saudi and to Texas as slaves. In Saudi, light-skinned slave owners had intermarried with their darker-skinned slaves. On the contrary, though white and black had intermingled in America, the intermingling was hardly within the bonds of matrimony. But in Saudi even though slavery still existed, there had never been the American South's revulsion to dark skin.

Islam was colour-blind. Saudi was not segregated according to skin colour.

As Faisal had repeatedly failed in his efforts to understand this Southern preoccupation with race, he had searched his memory for similar racial shadings in Saudi. 'Allah yebaiyth wajhak – God whiten your face' – was what one Saudi said as a blessing to another. Back in Arabia lighter skin usually meant higher social status and was considered cosmetically more attractive. A father would probably not want to marry his beige-skinned daughter to a black-skinned man. And if a photographer expected to be paid for taking a flattering portrait of a tribesman, he was well advised to expose the negative in such a way that the man's skin looked several shades paler.

But compared to Texas, skin colour in Saudi was only a superficial consideration. Far more important was a man's status within his tribe, his wealth in camels or land, and – most important of all – his piety, generosity, and courage. In Saudi there was none of the South's ugly racial hatred. Faisal and the other Arabs enrolled here at the University were very careful not to provoke racial incidents. The Arabs kept to themselves; they shared off-campus apartments together, they cooked their own kebab and rice, and they tried not to use the segregated public transportation and rest rooms.

When Faisal first arrived in Texas, a Lebanese who had already spent three and a half-isolated years here working on his doctorate had tersely told him it was an insult when a Texan called you a 'nigger' or 'wetback.' Texans despised 'coloured' skin on Negros, Mexicans, or even Arabs. Faisal then had gone into the bathroom ad taken a long, speculative, and merciless look in the mirror. His skin definitely was not white, or pink or beige or grey. Or red, like one of the sunburnt Americans who worked in Saudi. But neither was it black or dark brown. As far as he could judge the colour of his skin was a dark gold.

His skin was neither darker nor lighter than that of the other members of the Al-Murrah, an ancient, noble 'sharif' tribe of brave proud warriors. He remembered his grandfather,

Hassan, in rich and beautiful Arabic, delivering a long and ornate history of the tribe in Arabia, the cradle of life.

In the beginning of time, when Allah created the heavens and the earth, the Garden of Eden had lain not far away, just twelve miles off the peninsula on the island of Bahrain. There Eve plucked the fruit, and sin was born. Adam and Eve were expelled from the garden of earthly delights, and they were the first to wander as the Bedouin still wander on the parched earth of Arabia. Eve, who was the mother of not only Cain and Abel but of pain and suffering, finally died when it was written that she must die. She was buried in what is now the Saudi city of Jeddah, where it is still possible to visit her moldering tomb.

Grandfather Hassan had recited the genealogy from father to son, through all the centuries, from Adam to the Patriarch Abraham to Yam, the father of all the People of Murrah. For millennia, for as far back as man and memory, the fathers of the al-Murrah had been lords of the desert. For millennia, for as far back as man had history, their ancestors had ranked high in the hierarchy of the noblest and freest and bravest of the Arabian tribes. Hassan chronicled Al-Murrah victories in raids and in battles. He recounted the valour of its warriors and the eloquence of its poets and the wisdom of its chiefs. He extolled its piety and its fiercely devout defence of Islam.

But as Faisal continued to look in the mirror, he had come to the reluctant and startling and insulting conclusion that even though he and his family were first among equals in Saudi, here in Texas, he would be considered inferior, contemptible, and 'coloured.'

He supposed he might have made friends among the Negro or Mexican students, but there were none in his classes. It was rumoured that the oil companies had made special arrangements with the college so that the Arabs could enroll. The Arabs debated among themselves whether it was a blessing or a curse that they had been allowed to study here. Some transferred to colleges in California or the North as quickly as they could.

Faisal had resisted the impulse to transfer. This program in petroleum engineering was one of the best in the world. It was important to the welfare of his people that he understood everything about the ocean of oil under his country; where to find it, how to transport it, and how to make the most money from it. He could almost see a divine purpose in studying the oil.

On the western coast of Arabia, where the Prophet Muhammad had lived and preached and died, lay Mecca and Medina, the two holiest shrines of Islam. On the eastern coast of Arabia, where Aramco had dug in, lay what might be the richest oil reserves in the world. There could be a holy connection between Saudi as the font of Islam and Saudi as the well of oil. If he continued to study hard, if he learned all the Americans could teach him, if he made himself even smarter and tougher and more imaginative than the Americans, perhaps someday he might be able t help the brotherhood of Muslims make the most of that God-given oil.

Faisal had nothing against Aramco and the Americans like Mr. Jim. He had not begrudged repaying the Americans for discovering and developing the oil. But in the Middle Eastern bonanza years since 1948, the Western oil companies had made nearly ten billion dollars in pure profits. Surely the Arab debt to the West was more than paid in full.

He agreed with his fellow students from Iraq, Iran, Lebanon, and Kuwait that the oil companies must be nationalized. He considered himself a man more of religion than of politics, yet he too, along with the educated elite of his generation, had been swept along the currents of Arab nationalism.

He was at the university in Cairo in 1952 when Gamal Abdul Nasser deposed the Egyptian king who was even more corrupt and extravagant than the Saudi royal family. Over the next few years Faisal had often listened to Nasser speak of Arab pride and Arab nationalism ad Arab socialism. And just this summer, when Nasser had nationalized the Suez Canal, Faisal had cut out a photograph of his hero from a magazine and taped it to the wall above his desk.

Sometimes he thought that what his own country needed was a hero like Nasser. Faial was begging to resent the nepotism and greed of the House of Saud. Only fifty years ago, the Al-Saud had been only one of the many warring tribes of Arabia. When grandfather Hassan was a boy, the Saudis had been run off their ancient tribal lands and forced to live in impoverished exile in Kuwait. But since then, the star of the House of Saud had risen perhaps too high. The princes spent lavishly in the capitals of Europe while at home destitute tribesman all but starved to death in the desert. Faisal did not forget that the oil that made true kings of the House of Saud came from the ancient territory of the Al-Murrah.

He had admired old King Abdul Aziz. But the desert lion who had renamed all Arabia for his tribe had died three years ago, and his son Saud was the worst of his cubs. Saud was weak, corrupt, and degenerate, too fond of his women and his wine. He could also abuse his people. When workers in the Saudi oil fields had gone on strike for higher wages and better working conditions, King Saud had crushed them by calling out troops and imposing martial law. Then, just this past June, a visit by King Saud to Dhahran had triggered a spontaneous walkout by Aramco's Arab workers. But the king had refused to meet with the strikers and instead had ordered a total ban on all union and political activity.

Faisal knew what was behind the crackdown. The king, and the Americans of Aramco, were terrified that what had happened in Iran over the past few years could happen in Saudi.

When Muhammad Mossadegh, a popular firebrand, had been swept to power in Iran in 1951, his first public act had been to nationalize the British-run oil industry. But the British had withdrawn their crews from the oil fields, and production had come to a standstill because there were no skilled native crews. Then the British embargoed Iranian oil so successfully that Mossadegh couldn't even sell his crude oil for one tenth of its former value. Anti-British riots broke out over all over Iran, the Shah fled the country, and eventually the American Central Intelligence Agency stepped in to bring back the Shah and to give a new consortium of Western powers control over Iranian oil. Dr. Mossadegh, the fiery, aristocratic, European-educated Prime Minister, who despised the pretensions of the Shah dynasty, was overthrown, but remained an Iranian hero. Faisal thought the Saudi government had chosen to learn the wrong lessons from Iran. Instead of banning all domestic political activity, the Saudi government should be concentrating on how best to take control of its own natural resources. It was madness to nationalize an industry unless there were skilled native workers to replace the foreigners, and it was foolhardy to expect that one lone oil-producing country could dictate new terms to the powerful Western oil-consuming nations.

The radical government of Iran had been bankrupted and brought to its knees because the West had stuck together. Instead of suffering from a shortage of oil, the West had simply brought more oil from Saudi Arabia and Kuwait and Iraq. Faisal thought the lessons of all this were obvious. The Islamic nations would never have a chance to get the better of the West unless the Islamic nations acted in concert.

Yet Faisal was troubled. He had no personal axe to grind with the West. He was grateful to Mr. Jim's country for the opportunities it had given him. And yet sometimes Faisal was ambivalent about even these opportunities. Life had had more certainties for his grandfather's and even his father's generation. He worried that his own grandsons might reproach him for not reasserting the old values while there was still time, for it could be that man lost more than he gained by turning his back resolutely on the past. He wished it were possible to pick and choose only what one wanted of 'progress' and thus avert what he sometimes saw as the decay and decadence of the West. Often Faisal had longed for the purity and peace and the simplicity of life in the desert as his grandfather had lived it. He wondered if the good times had ended or only begun in the lifetime of his grandfather Hassan.

Faisal felt a protective tenderness toward the unborn generations of all Arabs and all Muslims. He feared sometimes that the allure of the libertine values of the West would triumph over the arduous religious and tribal disciplines of Islam. When he himself had tried to strike a balance between the two worlds, he had discovered the discomfort of belonging to neither. He found himself, heart, and soul, to be either totally Western or totally Eastern. Perhaps it didn't matter which side he chose so long as he could become a true believer.

He wished ardently that he could spare future generations the confusion of trying to reconcile East and West. He supposed one answer would be to wed the religious values of Islam to the scientific technologies of the West. But wishing the best both worlds for his sons and the sons of his sons would not guarantee it for them.

Faisal's dream was to use the money from the oil to make his people as strong and as free and as moral as the Prophet Muhammad had wanted them to be. He was aware of the arrogance and the awesome ambition of his great dream, and so he did not confide it even to his Muslim roommates. He had long ago trained himself to keep silent about his innermost thoughts. When he home to Saudi, he would have to worry about the long arm of the secret police. If he wanted to rise in the Saudi oil industry, he would have to keep his ideas about oil and money and Islamic power and the corruptions of the House of Saud to himself.

There were rumours of financial crisis in the kingdom. Even millions of dollars in increased oil revenues had not been able to keep pace with the profligate spending of King Saud, seven years after taking power. He had mortgaged the once bright future of the oil-rich kingdom. His extravagances were a page out of 'Tales from the Arabian Nights.' He had taken a dislike to his newly built, eight-million-dollar Nasriyah Palace, ordered bulldozers to level it, and then, on the same site, built another even more grandiose at a cost of twenty million dollars. He had stocked and restocked his harem with foreign and native ladies, and it was said he sired a hundred children.

He had amused himself on trips to Europe buying up entire inventories of jewelry stores and china patterns and couture designers. He bought airplanes and stereo equipment and enough flashing neon lights to make his palace garden light up the desert like Las Vegas.

Still the king had continued his mad sprees, and a percentage of all that spending had swollen the Swiss bank accounts of advisers and assistants and chamberlains and fawning flunkies from Egypt and Lebanon and Palestine and Britain and Germany, who had all descended on Saudi Arabia like a cloud of flies on a freshly killed carcass. King Saud ignored the advice of his brothers and instead made policy by consulting his former chauffer, whom he made the controller of royal budgets. He dabbled disastrously in foreign policy, and the Arab world was scandalized when it was revealed he had offered Syria a four-million-dollar bribe to sabotage its planned union with Egypt and even, some whispered, to assassinate President Nasser.

But worst of all, King Saud had brought the kingdom to the brink of bankruptcy. He owed ninety-two million dollars to Chase Manhattan and other New York banks, and the Saudi riyal had fallen sharply against the dollar.

An impending shake-up in the royal family was strongly rumoured. If someone didn't do something about King Saud – and soon – what had happened in Egypt nearly eighty years ago could happen before another season passed in Saudi. When the extravagances of Khedive Ishmael had bankrupted Egypt in the late nineteenth century, Britain had stepped in to safeguard its extensive investments, and Egypt had become a glorified British colony. Faisal fretted that the pretext of a similar Saudi bankruptcy might soon have a caravan of American tanks on the camel tracks outside Riyadh. "Make no mistake," Faisal said.

The American oil industry would tolerate the Saudi monarchy in power for only as long as king and court served American interests. If the Saudis s couldn't run their country in a stable manner, then the Americans would take off the velvet gloves and come out in the open and run it for them.

To forestall such a catastrophe, the rumour was that an intra-palace coup was being planned on behalf of Crown Prince Faisal. He was Saud's half-brother and not only the heir apparent and the foreign minister, but also most assuredly the sanest head in Riyadh. King Saud would be allowed to continue to rule in name only, but Prince Faisal would be the real power. He would put King Saud on a strict budget, he would stop the mad cycle of extravagance, he would make all the hard choices that must be made to avert American intervention.

And soon afterwards, the dour, smart King Faisal eclipsed King Saud. The national budget was balanced by young bureaucrats with fancy college degrees and the Saudis assumed control of half the assets of Aramco. Saudi Arabia squared off against Egypt in the Yemeni Civil war.

These were the benign years when the Western gods of development and technology and modernization secured long term Saudi visas, when progress seemed inevitable and without ambiguity, when armies of experts descended on Riyadh and Jeddah and Dhahran with their blueprints and their full-colour glossy brochures and their five-year plans that promised prosperity and longer lives and the best of everything.

These were the believing years, when for the first time ever in Arabia all seemed possible, when new schools and hospitals opened their doors to the ignorant and the sick, when electricity and telephones and radios and television sets became an everyday matter, when trucks replaced camels, when pilgrims from all over the world flew to Mecca on airplanes in a matter of hours instead of the years it used to take some to arrive by foot and by boat and by slow caravan. These were the naïve years before the great arrogance began, before self-interest quickened and honed minds realized just what economic and political power could come with this oil – their oil – not Aramco's oil but Saudi's oil.

These were the boom years, the years before the conservation, the wildly productive years of straining growth, when bargain basement barrels of black gold, pumped from the rich new fields, increased from the thousands to the tens of thousands to the hundreds of thousands to the millions of barrels per day. These were the pauper years when the Western companies capriciously slashed and slashed again, oil's posted price of less than two dollars a barrel, when the kingdom seemed not to carry a grudge for its sharply decreased revenue, when the Saudis were docile , resigned, and inscrutable, when the Arabs merely sighed and made the best of this as their ancestors had sighed and made the best of whatever calamities Allah had sent them.

But in that lonely, drowsy, sultry Texas summer, there was no one to share either Faisal's dreams or his fears. Until June he had been living in an apartment with a Kuwaiti, two Iraqis, and another Aramco scholarship student from Saudi. But two of them had graduated and the others had gone home for the summer. Faisal was sticking it out here alone so he could get his degree at the end of summer, then enroll this fall in a management program at the Massachusetts Institute of Technology. The more Faisal studied oil, the more convinced he became that what mattered was not the physical extraction of the oil from the ground but the engineering of the prices and the power of the industry itself. In Texas he was learning the nuts and bolts of producing petroleum. But in Massachusetts he would begin to study the economic potential of that oil for his country.

Faisal tried not to stare at the Twiggy-like white woman who was coming toward him on the narrow sidewalk. He knew by now that it was dangerous to stare at the white women of Texas, even when they wore provocative clothing, even when they looked at him in a very seductive way. This particular woman was wearing a low-cut almost diaphanous white blouse, a wide red belt that accentuated her small breasts, a full red skirt that billowed over slim flashing bare legs. Faisal thought her tongue flicked obscenely as she savoured every sensual lick of her strawberry ice cream cone.

Reluctantly he tore his eyes away. Besides, he did not want this woman who was as bony as a starving camel at the end of a caravan's forced march across the desert. Faisal had been surprised that so many American women were so lean. America was such a rich country, and there seemed such an overabundance of food here. He couldn't understand why so many of the women looked half-starved. He doubted they were all suffering from some dreadful wasting sickness. Perhaps it was just another Western quirk. Or it may even be that these Americans were poorer than they pretended. It was possible they couldn't afford to feed their women.

Faisal's Arab friends talked incessantly, obsessively, continuously about American women. They would have liked them plumper, but they praised their straight light hair, and most of all they increasingly speculated about their apparent sexual availability. What man with any juice in him could avoid thinking constantly about sex here? Women parade around half-naked, billboards displayed ripe white flesh, sex was everywhere here, everywhere.

Yet in Texas it would have been very dangerous if the dark-skinned Arabs had dared to touch the white men's women. They tried instead to be content simply to ogle all that fabulous bare flesh. But then Ali, one of the Arabs from Baghdad, who had porcelain-white skin, had dated Judi, a coed from the Midwest. A very disappointed Ali had reported back that even though this girl dressed like a strumpet, she wouldn't let him do much more than kiss her on the lips. After a few frustrating dates, Ali was glad to return to his favourite whore at the Mexican brothel on the outskirts of town.

Faisal and the others tried, and failed, to fit Ali's experience into some elaborate theory about sexual mores here in America. It couldn't be true that American girls were a tease. For the thousandth time, Faisal wondered how it could be possible that American brothers and fathers did not do more to protect the innocence of their young women. Didn't they care? Didn't they lover their daughters and sisters? Didn't they want to make certain they were not hurt by predatory men? Didn't they have any conception of family honour?

Faisal did not like to believe Americans were as godless and immoral as they appeared to be. Even those that called themselves Christians and who went to their churches every Sunday still did not appear to make their religion a way of life. He did not envy these Americans. Life, for them, must have no certainties. Life for them must be empty and flat and joyless and terrifying.

He looked back in disapproval at the retreating figure of the woman wearing a low-cut white blouse and a full red skirt. He watched her wiggle her behind very shamelessly. He shook his head, then looked ahead of him on the street where a pack of obviously drunken cowboys were making fools of themselves.

Faisal looked up at the sky again. The yellow was fading to grey now. Surely in ten minutes or so, even the most devout Muslims would agree that the sun was down, and it was time to break the fast. It was not supposed to be easy to keep this strict fast of Ramadan, commemorating the sacred month when Allah revealed the Holy Qur'an to the Prophet Muhammad in the desert.

A touch of the desert gives depth to living. Some of our cousin 'Yehudi's' prophets like John the Baptist were also men from the desert. And the 'Yehudi' nation itself was forged in the desert. The desert is the place where life is stripped bare, and we can clearly see the issues of God and the world. In its sparse environment pared clean by the wind and corroding sand, man is thrown into total dependence upon God.

It was from the desert that the 'Nazrani' holy writer John was shown the seductive and repulsive power of the materialistic world system, Babylon. You are only safe in the marketplace if you are at home in the desert. Those who speak in the marketplace what they have perceived in the desert will be subversives to their world order. They will swim against the tide. They attack the status quo. The 'tolerant' world will not tolerate them. There must be a touch of the desert about our lives, a quality of life which writes an incarnate question mark against the values of the world we live in.

It seemed to Faisal that the lunar month of Ramadan was the hardest of all to observe when it fell during the long hot days of August. The first rays of sunrise had crept over the humpy Texas hills at three o'clock this morning. It was now nearly seven-thirty. For the past sixteen and a half hours, Faisal had not so much as swallowed his own spit. He looked finally, up at the sky. The last rays of the sunlight had been extinguished from the sky. Today's Ramadan fast was over. It was permitted, now for him to eat and drink.

Faisal was so parched he was dizzy as he out one foot unsteadily in front of the other. At times like this, when his physical strength was at a low ebb, he could almost shut his eyes and believe himself to be not here in this alien country but home. This damp, humid heat was like Saudi. This heavy, grainy dust hanging almost visible in the air was like Saudi. This sapping, draining tiredness he felt all through his limbs was like Saudi.

He licked his lips slowly as he looked up at the once yellow sky, where dust clouds all but hid the spreading reddish bruise of the setting sun. For during this Islamic Ramadan month of fasting, if he were walking down the main street of a Saudi oasis right now, he most assuredly would be the only man in sight. From dawn to dusk during this holy month, life even in the bustling towns of Arabia came close to a standstill. For two or three weeks they couldn't post or receive letters or go to the bank until Ramadan was officially over and they had celebrated the 'Eid-el-Fitr' feast and returned from their desert camp back to the family compound in Al-Khobar.

Every Ramadan afternoon a peculiar almost breathless silence would fall during the final minutes before it was permissible to break the fast, As the desert heat seemed to burn away life's trivial surface, the breathless silence of Ramadan seemed to drown out all the voices but the implacable ones inside your head; sometimes they are voices from deep dense dreams, or just voices tinged with strong religious emotions.

No veiled women would be seen carrying buckets to the wells, no robed and scarved men would be seen lounging outside their houses, no camels or donkeys or trucks or cars would be moving down the shadowless streets. Everyone would be inside preparing, with many thanks to God – 'El-Hamdulillah!' – to break the fast with prayer, water, and food.

Faisal missed the camaraderie of shared Ramadan sacrifice. When everyone within sight and sound was languishing through the rigors of the fast, it was not so difficult to abstain from all food and drink during the daylight hours. It was unthinkable, in Saudi, during the light of a Ramadan day, for anyone to eat or drink in public.

In Saudi, during Ramadan, not even an American Christian dared to eat an apple or smoke a cigarette as he walked down a street. The swaggering 'mutawiyah,' the religious police, who prowled the streets with their long heavy canes made sure that did not happen. They have been known to beat Saudi men on the spot for missing a call to prayer or even smoking a cigarette.

Chapter 17

After the oil companies had slashed the posted price of oil in the late 50s, Faisal and other Western educated Saudis had been instrumental in forming the Organisation of Petroleum Exporting Countries – OPEC – to pressure the companies to restore the price of oil to its former levels. Now Faisal was always dashing off not only for OPEC organizing conferences but also to meet with Arabs and Iranians up and down the Gulf. Faisal was one of Tariki's boys. Abdulla Tariki was the controversial head of the Saudi Ministry of Petroleum, and the nemesis of Western oil interests in the middle East. It had been Tariki's idea to bind the Third World oil-producing nations together in OPEC, and he was doing all he could to radicalize the Saudi oil industry.

He wanted more Saudis in higher positions, he wanted more Saudi control at all levels of Aramco affairs, he wanted Saudis involved in transporting, refining, and marketing of oil once it left Arabia, and he wanted Saudis to renegotiate Aramco's concession territory. Faisal was advised by Jim Lawrence to be careful with Tariki, that he was on the way out and that King

Faisal thought he was a revolutionary. But so long as Faisal kept at least a little distance between himself and Tariki now was the time to join the government team. That was where the future lay. Before long the Saudis would be calling the shots and all those big cheeses at Aramco would be glorified flunkies.

"That'll be the day," Faisal doubted.

"You'll live to see it, I think." A note of satisfaction swept into Jim's voice.

He had no illusions about Standard Oil and Mobil and the other oil giants who were behind Aramco.

"Mark my words, there will be a day of reckoning. Aramco has made a bloody fortune out of Saudi Arabia. Oh, I know the company built hospitals and schools here, and jumped when the kings and the princes have said to jump, and filled a lot of numbered royal bank accounts in Switzerland. But all that's been too little, too late. The American oil companies have robbed Saudi blind for nearly thirty years. They've had unlimited amounts of incredibly cheap Saudi Arabian oil at their disposal since my Number Two well came in. But the oil's going to run out some day at this rate. It's a real shame that the Arabs weren't paid a fair price for the oil, and that simple conservation wasn't practiced before it was too late." Jim sighed. "There will be hell to pay when the Arabs wise up. Already it's started with your OPEC. However, the sticking point is whether the Arabs and the Iranians and all the others will even be able to make a united front for this or any other reason."

When Faisal has finished his studies in America, he decided to spend a little time in France before turning home to Saudi Arabia. He first stopped over in Paris and hired a taxi to take him to the Saudi embassy. In French he gave his order: 'Avenue Hoche. Cinque, avenue Hoche. L'ambassade de l'Arabie Saoudite.'

It was raining and Faisal stifled a yawn as he watched the taxi's windscreen wipers hypnotically beat back and forth in the steady drizzle. His driver was a wooly-haired expatriate from Tunisia. Instead of the usual static-filled rock music on the radio, this driver played a wailing cassette of whiny Arab love songs. Faisal didn't much care for the caterwauling music on the driver's cassette. But over and over the driver had played the same scratchy tape with the volume turned up full. As they plied their way slowly but surely towards the embassy, the Arab singer Um Kulthum had shrieked and whined and wailed about every bit of pain and loss in her long and miserable life.

Faisal watched the driver's dark mobile face in the mirror. When Um Kulthum sobbed her most melodramatic chorus about perfidious love, the driver would clench the steering wheel and moan and shake his head and all but wipe his eyes. It was as if he was already inside the Middle East – on wheels.

The taxi swung around the arc de Triomphe and in to Avenue Hoche. It pulled up to the elegant three-story chancellery with its fluttering green Saudi flag with an emblem of palm trees and crossed swords. Faisal blanched at the heavy grillwork that barred the windows and the guard who patrolled the sidewalk with machine guns. As he looked down the street there were boisterous French children shouting behind the ornate gilded gate of the Parc Monceau.

Faisal left the embassy after about an hour in the same taxi that brought him to the chancellery. He went to a luxury hotel in the heart of Paris, facing the Opera House and between the Louvre Museum and the gardens of the Palais-Royal. Also checking in at the reception desk was a very attractive vivacious French girl, perhaps nineteen or twenty years old, whom he watched speaking in quite tolerable Arabic to the Tunisian driver who was bringing in Faisal's luggage.

Faisal's and this girl's eyes locked as she gave him a most seductive smile. Faisal felt something he'd never allowed himself to feel as a thrill of strong sexual desire coursed through him. Her name, he quickly found out, was Nicole Juppe. She'd just come up to Paris to do some shopping. She had spent her early years in Algeria where her father had been a rich plantation owner before De Gaulle's intervention allowed Algeria to gain independence.

Nicole made Faisal somehow feel at home, not like those so called 'roses' of the sickly-pale white Texas world he'd been trying to obliterate from his memory. As Nicole sat down on one of the plush sofas of the reception lounge, she leaned back and crossed her long lithe legs and tossed her long thick hair. She had the feeling Faisal was watching her.

She tapped a cigarette on the tabletop, and she sighed a soft, troubled little sigh. She then recrossed her legs and re-arranged her hair and pouted her lips for a smoke. She lit her cigarette and inhaled. Nicole had rejected the boring certainties of her parent's life and longed to take risks, do deeds, live her life to the hilt. Ever since she could remember, she had nursed dreams of a life of extraordinary adventure. She thought that if she had been born a boy, she might have become a soldier of fortune or an explorer or a spy.

Nicole caught her breath and stared at Faisal's sensual, ascetic face. He had a strong beak nose and lustrous wavy black hair. He looked brooding and vulnerable and tortuously, intensely, romantic. Her imagination ran riot. It was so easy to imagine him in an Arab robe and head scarf, riding his camel over the sand as he hunted gazelles. The corners of her mouth turned up in a welcoming smile, and she couldn't stop staring at his extraordinary eyes.

He looked like some sort of sexually magnetic saint, maybe painted long ago by El Greco. Was El Greco, she wondered dizzily, an Arab or a Greek? Perhaps a Moor? She tried to picture Faisal as Othello. She couldn't help laughing out loud at such a giddy chain of thought. The lightness of her laughter hung in the heavy air of the afternoon.

Encouraged, Faisal came and sat by her and spoke tentatively to her in Arabic. Faisal had always been proud and quick tempered; but after his unhappy experience in Texas, his olive skin was translucently thin. He was not going to force himself on any Western woman-not he, not now, not ever. He recalled how he had been so lonely and suspicious of Texans and Americans. He looked longingly at this pretty young French girl. Would he have come to sit by her like this if Nicole were not the sort of girl he had been dreaming of for the past few years? Faisal wished he had been content to watch her from afar. He told himself he should never have assumed, just because she spoke some Arabic, that she was any different from the rest.

Perhaps she didn't like Arabs and was prejudice against dark skin. Perhaps she was racist and imperialist and every other evil Faisal was beginning to believe Americans and Westerners were born to be. He was furious at himself for courting another Western rebuff, and he vowed never to repeat this mistake. "So sorry to intrude, and he vowed never to repeat this mistake. "So sorry, mademoiselle." He rose to finish making his escape.

It would have stopped there, before it even began, if it hadn't been Nicole's great belief in the rightness of her instincts. Without stopping to consider what she was doing, she reached out a hand and bravely touched his arm.

"Wait."

As he turned to look warily at her, she wondered at her impulse to reach out to him. Solemnly she searched Faisal's face. His was not, she thought, a happy face. She thought she could read traces of hurt or disillusion in his wounded eyes.

Nicole felt a wave of tenderness for this young man wash over her. Perhaps more purely and more simply than she ever was to feel anything again in her life she wanted happiness and good fortune and no tragedy ever to befall him.

She wished it were possible that she herself could bestow all that good fortune on him. All her instincts told her that here before her stood a good man. She was certain, suddenly, as if she had been gifted with second sight, that if she wanted it, if she dared to want it – this good and decent man could play a major role in her life. Tentatively she smiled at him.

"As you like." He would stand here and exchange cold politeness with her for as long as she liked. His anger evaporated as he watched her. She was beautiful and, he supposed, she was rich. She seemed as lonely as he was. Her eyes were as guileless as a child's – lovely pale light foreign eyes. Such gentle, trusting, believing, innocent eyes. How could her parents let a vulnerable young girl like this go off alone in a big city like Paris? A dishonorable man could come along to take advantage of the innocence of this lovely girl. Again, Faisal was reassured that the Saudi way with women was better than the Western way.

Nicole looked into Faisal's wild-animal eyes and thought wryly how all her life she had yearned for her own princely Saudi 'shaykh,' and now that she had one's undivided attention, she couldn't even make small talk. It occurred to her finally that he was still standing, and so she moved a used coffee cup and asked him to sit down.

"Coffee?" she smiled. "They have Turkish coffee here. I always have it."

A slow smile spread from his eyes to his lips. "Turkish coffee?" He snapped his fingers. "You mean 'Arab' coffee?" He laughed. "I get us some, yes?" He was still laughing as he leapt up. He looked so different when he laughed.

She wished she could say or do something here, now, forever, to keep this young man happy and laughing.

Her wish came true. Faisal was still laughing as he came back with two tiny cups of 'Arab' coffee, two glasses of water, and two dainty French pastries all expertly balanced on a tray. "I have a very sweet tooth, so these cakes."

They both laughed but there was a giddiness to their laughter. But she shook her head at the pastry. "No fattening cake for me."

"Eat! No worry! A girl like you – so beautiful! – you should eat, enjoy." He handed her a fork. "For me you must eat."

Instead, Nicole pulled a cigarette from her pack. She leaned back, she crossed her legs, she tossed her hair. She put the cigarette between her lips and waited for him to light it the way men did in the movies. Instead, he frowned, reached over, and plucked the cigarette from between her lips and snapped it in two.

"No cigarettes. Not for *you.*"

"No?" If at this moment this fabulous man had swept her into his arms, she thought she might be his forever. He took her breath away.

"No. Smoking is very bad, especially for women. You must never smoke. He picked up a fork and handed it to her. "You must eat. For me, yes? He beamed at her.

Meekly she ate every bite of the pastry. When she had finished, she sighed, "That was good," She sipped the Arab coffee.

"May I call you Faisal?"

"But of course!"

"Tell me, Faisal, do they have coffee like this in Saudi?"

"Pardon?"

"At home. In Saudi? Do they have coffee there?"

"Do we have coffee? Arabs *invented* coffee! In Yemen, in Arabia, was the first coffee. Of course we have coffee! In the desert every day, every afternoon, every night – coffee, always coffee. First sound every morning – ping! – boy grinds coffee beans. First smell every morning – ah! – the coffee. And what coffee? Best coffee in all the world. Not like this coffee here; old, stale, flat. Coffee in Arabia is much more wonderful, you understand, yes?"

"Oh yes!" Radiantly she smiled. Finally, at long last, she was truly hearing about the land of her dreams. This boy, this wonderful handsome masterful boy, knew everything there was to know about Arabia. She would ask him to tell her all about it.

"The desert! You love the desert, don't you Faisal? It is really wonderful in the desert?"

"Ah!" His face was aglow. "Yes, Nicole. The desert, my desert, is a very wonderful. Can you imagine, for a moment, what it is to grow up with the infinities of the desert in your soul? It makes you a very private person."

"You'll tell me about, Saudi, Faisal? You'll tell me all about it?"

"You want to know about my country?"

"Oh, yes!"

He rose with decision. "So first I will get you another sweet cake. And then I will come back and tell you all about my country?"

"And coffee. Don't forget the Arab coffee."

He turned back to her. "I will forget nothing, Nicole. Always, for you, wonderful woman Nicole, I will remember everything."

A month later they travelled *together* in Nicole's sports car from Marseille to Cannes and the hot rich Riviera, which Nicole called the prettiest place in Europe. Faisal tucked Nicole's arm in his as they walked towards the beach.

Umbrellas stretched six deep, edge, for half a mile along the silvery beach. Bodies lay stretched out baking in the sun, hundreds to the acre, a perfect bed of heated brown flesh.

"They have ruined the place, ruined it," cried Nicole, as she surveyed the untidy scene.

They looked about. Two feet away was a mass of tangled brown limbs belonging to half a dozen boys and girls, the girls wearing nothing but minuscule G-string coloured cotton panties and miniscule coloured cotton bras, with their firm straining breasts almost popping out every time they shifted positions. Faisal could hardly tear his eyes off them.

Then there was, eighteen inches to the other side, a vast grey-haired lady, weary pallid flesh bulging out of a white cotton playsuit. Faisal didn't seem to notice her.

A newly arrived couple kept turning over and over on the sand like a pair of herrings grilling, as if they felt their pale skins to be a shame and a disgrace.

A colony of English kept to itself some hundreds of yards away.

Nicole and Faisal watched the children screaming and laughing in the unvarying blue waves. They watched groups of French adolescents flirt and roll each other over on the sand in a way which Faisal thought appallingly free. Nothing could have persuaded Faisal of the extreme respectability of these youngsters. He suspected them of shocking and complicated vices. Nicole though it incredible that in so few years they would be sorted by some powerful and comforting social process into decent, well-fed French couples, each so anxiously absorbed in the welfare of one, or perhaps two, small children.

They watched also, with admiration, the more hardened swimmers cleave out through the small waves into the sea beyond the breakwater with their masks, their air tubes, their frog's feet.

This is what all these hundreds of thousands of people along the coast had come for, to lie on the sand and receive the sun on their heating bodies, to receive, too, in small doses, the hot blue water which dried too stickily on them. The sea was very salty, and warm – smelling of a little more than salt and weed, for beyond the breakwater the town's sewers spilled into the sea, washing back into the inner bay rich deposits which dried on the perfumed oiled bodies of the happy bathers. This is what they had come for.

Faisal continued to hold on to Nicole and he reveled in the sensation of hovering over this lovely French girl. He still deluded himself that he was escorting her much as he would have shepherded protectively a sister or an aunt or a daughter back in Saudi. Even though Faisal's loving feelings were neither those of a brother nor those of a father, it still gave him great and gallant pleasure to know that he was watching over her with all the vigilance women deserved from the man who loved them.

Nicole gave his hand a squeeze as she smiled happily at him. When his liquid brown eyes flashed at her as they were doing now, she could read in them the assurance that he surely loved her. Yet still he had not told her so, still he had not asked her to marry him, still he had not even kissed her. Lord, she thought, these Arabs are slow. She brushed away the fleeting memory of her last French boyfriend Jacques who had been anything but slow. She hardly remembered Jacques anymore; but when she did it always with a shiver of sexual shame.

Nicole assumed that she and Faisal would marry before he went back to Paris and then home to Saudi. She had even consulted an atlas to begin planning their honeymoon across what she considered the romantic capitals of Europe. She drew a red line from Paris to Vienna to Florence and to Rome, and then circled Saudi Arabia in a giant red heart.

Nicole sighed and smiled sweetly up at Faisal. Yet there was calculation in her eyes and her smile and the way she clung to him with her breast snuggled up against his arm. She was determined Faisal was finally going to kiss her today.

Even though they saw each other nearly every day in Marseilles, he hardly ever touched her. She ached sometime with the suspense of waiting. When they walked as close together as they were now, she could hardly keep from throwing herself into his arms. She wondered why his not touching her excited her more than if he had groped her with the insistent roving hands of every French boy she had gone out with. She quivered sometimes with the wanting of him and he not quite touching her.

The first time she had felt the heat of his nearness had been by accident on the metro. The crowded car was making a sharp turn near the St. Lazare station when it jerked almost off the tracks. She lost her balance and was thrown against him, he caught her so she would not fall, and for one moment only she was pressed full-length against him. As he held her, they stared longingly into each others eyes, and for one heady instant he pulled her even closer. But when the metro car came out of the turn, they had broken apart and looked everywhere but at each other until they had passed their stop.

The following week he had finally reached out and touched her deliberately as they were cutting through the gardens of the Palais-Royal. He had pulled her closer to him and given her a chaste peck on the cheek.

Faisal was again assailed by the nagging litany of sensible reasons why he couldn't have Nicole. He was certain a cousin bride had already been chosen for him to marry on his return to Saudi. He and Nicole would be doomed by too many differences in outlook and culture. Nicole was good-hearted and he loved her, but she was a romantic girl who had dreamed too many dreams of Saudi. He greatly doubted that this sheltered, privileged Christian girl could come camp with him for evermore in the desert, or find a place for herself among the women of his tribe, or ever accept the mask and veil and seclusion.

Even with the best of intentions, even with the most endless and adaptable of loves, the two of them would have to endure too many heartbreaks. It was madness to love her. Yet reciting his reservations did not alter the fact that he adored this impetuous, vibrant, voluptuous young French woman. Faisal sighed. He wished he could marry her and raise a family with her and walk beside her like this all his days.

Nicole interpreted his sigh as a declaration of love. As she matched her strides to his, she reveled in being in step with him, of swinging the weight of her body exactly in synchronization with his. Nicole was so happy she hummed a few bars of an Edith Piaf song – No Regrets – as they walked along in their own private world of wonders.

"You sing. Never before have I heard you sing. You are so happy, Nicole, that you sing?"

She tried to tease him with some Arabic words. "Wallah' – by God – she said, "you make me so 'masrourah' – happy – that I want to sing."

"Yes?" He laughed at her adorable mock pidgin Arabic. "Then 'wallah,' you must sing for me. You must sing for me a song."

"Everyone says I have a terrible voice and that I'm tone deaf – no laughing matter! They say that I never sing in tune and that even when I try to hum or la-la-la a familiar tune the tune is unrecognizable. So there!" Nicole was suddenly self-conscious. "Besides, I though music was 'haram' – forbidden. I thought good Saudi Muslims weren't allowed to listen to music!"

He shrugged, sick for once, about what good Saudi Muslims were and were not allowed to do. He did not feel like explaining to her the significant differences between one man or one woman's singing a song and Tom Jones or Elvis Presley gyrating his pelvis on stage. He did not even care to educate her about ancient Arab songs that were musical poems of love. He merely wanted the simple pleasure of this woman, who he was increasingly beginning to regard as 'his' woman, singing him a song.

"Sing, Nicole." It was not a request but a command. "Sing to me."

Sometimes in the past week or two, lying on her bed, she had entertained herself with wild fantasies of Faisal in the role of the Saudi 'shaykh' and herself the willing, white-skinned, conquered infidel slave girl. Sometimes she was an odalisque lolling on silky divans in the harem. Sometimes she was the booty in a desert raid by savage rival tribes. Never was she anything as humdrum as Nicole Juppe, the daughter of an ex-plantation owner in Algeria.

Lying on her bed she had thrilled to her fantasies of a masterful man commanding submissive women. Yet now, when Faisal had finally given her an order, even though it was a command as innocent as singing a song, Nicole balked. Who was *he* to tell her to sing? To tell her to do anything? She assured herself she would do as *she* pleased, not as *he* ordered. She most certainly would not sing.

But when he asked her again, this time it was not so much a command as a plea. "You will not sing for me?" He sensed that he probably should not say what he was about to say, and that he would be leading her on if he said it. But Faisal took a deep breath and plunged ahead.

"At home, in the desert, a woman who feels a certain way for a man will sing for him."

Immediately her interest soared. If this was in fact a mating rite leading inevitably to their marriage, she would most certainly raise her off-key voice in song. She would do the high-kicking 'can-can' dance, would tap dance, or even sing operatic arias, if that meant she would thereby more quickly become his wife. Nicole laughed out loud at the picture that conjured up. An instant later their lips touched as Faisal was infected with the mood of her laughter. They kissed for a long time, Nicole pressing herself closer and closer to him, wanting him to kiss her everywhere and anywhere.

...

Nicole snatched the telephone off the cradle at its first ring. "Faisal? Finally! See you soon!"

She sped form the telephone on the hallway of their house in Marseilles back into her room to collect her purse and raincoat. Then she paused to look herself over on more time in the full-length mirror beside her desk.

She had decided to make tonight the night.

Anxiously she checked to see if she had lipstick smudged on her teeth, if her hair rippled just so on her shoulders, if her white slip was hanging below her red dress. Faisal liked her in bright, reds, oranges, purples – every colour her mother had always told her was worn only by tarty girls.

Faisal still kept his hands mostly off her. He would have to start moving fast if he intended to marry her, and Nicole had begun to despair that Faisal had neither the inclination nor the ability to move that fast. Nicole frowned at herself in the mirror. She had never imagined that her one true love would be the coy one. Every time she and Faisal were beginning to draw closer, he retreated. Yet Nicole never allowed herself to doubt for long that he loved her and wanted to take her back to Saudi as his wife.

When she asked him to marry her, his answer would be to sweep her into his arms and kiss her on the lips, on her eyes, at her temples. Then they would go off to celebrate their engagement, and it would all be perfect. She would have to break the news gently to her parents who had no inkling of what was afoot and who would probably not be overjoyed.

He hadn't asked her to marry him because he was shy or uncertain of how to proceed here in this alien Western culture, or because he was as slow-moving about courtship as he was about everything else. She would love him forever, but sometimes he was so slow she felt like jabbing his backside with one of the oversized hat pins she got from Paris.

Nicole stared doubtfully at herself in the mirror. Should she ask him to marry her? Was it now or never? She smiled tremulously at herself in the mirror, and then she crossed her fingers and went to meet her destiny.

She got into her car and drove to their rendezvous, a Lebanese restaurant in the heart of the city. They had eaten there before.

But Nicole never arrived.

As Faisal waited impatiently, he heard a crash some five hundred yards from the restaurant. A sports car and an articulated lorry loaded with freight from the port had been involved in an unequal crash with the sports car disappearing under the articulated lorry. Faisal's worst fears were soon confirmed as he approached the scene of the crash. The sports car was Nicole's and she had been killed instantly.

Faisal was very distraught and badly shaken; he couldn't help thinking that it was all Allah's judgement on him for his intended submission to Nicole's wish that they get married. He moved slowly away from the nightmare of the crash like a sleepwalker.

"Nicole! Nicole! I love you!" He heard his choked voice mutter.

He took the next available plane back to Saudi Arabia. The month of the 'hajj' had already begun. He would make the pilgrimage to Mecca for spiritual comfort, guidance, and renewal.

Chapter 18

Faisal felt the itch of the rough simple cotton he had wound around his waist and thrown over his shoulder against his skin. He was wearing the costume of the consecrated pilgrim bound for Mecca: two seamless lengths of white cotton, the 'ihram,' the simple covering that the Patriarch Abraham had once worn. Faisal was bareheaded, in the pilgrim's garb that symbolized piety, the righteous search for peace and purity, and the renunciation of all profane worldly pleasures.

Faisal stood on the summit of Jebal el-Rahmah, the Mount of Mercy, one questing and troubled and believing man among a sea of more than one million of the faithful who had assembled from Indonesia and Malaysia and India and Iran and China and America and Africa and every Arab nation of the Middle East.

They had come in 1970, this Islamic year of 1390, on the ninth day of the twelfth month, Dhu el-Hijjah, by foot and by camel and by horse and by donkey, by automobile and by moped and by truck, by boat and by airplane and by caravan, to perform one of the most sacred of the pillars of their faith.

Every Muslim, woman no less than man, is required, at least once before he dies, if he has enough money to afford it and is healthy enough to survive the rigors of the journey, to make this pilgrimage to the west coast of Saudi Arabia, here, to the holiest shrine in Islam.

Once in his life, as the highlight of his life, a Muslim must come here to God's country, on the fringe of the Arabian desert. On a day even more joyful than the day of the birth of his first-born son, a Muslim must make a pilgrimage here to where the Prophet Muhammad lived and was given the World of God as revealed in the Holy Qur'an. Here in Mecca all the races –brown men, black men, yellow men, white men – pray with one trembling, rapturous voice in the eternal brotherhood of the saved on the Plain of Abraham.

Faisal stood for the second time in his life among the believers making the 'hajj' to the Mount of Mercy. He and his brother Salim had come here first as boys, on camelback, for a pilgrimage if grace and dedication. Their grandfather had wanted their first glorious glimpse of Mecca to come after weeks of arduous camping in the desert. He wanted to burn the old ways into their memory. He wanted them to come as their Bedouin ancestors had always come, dusty and parched and thirsty for salvation. Faisal could never forget catching his breath at first sight of the holy city. They had come upon it suddenly by night. At the crest of a perilous ridge of dark desolate mountains, Faisal had stood transfixed by Mecca.

Its minarets, domes, and golden gates had been lit by lights of a green and blue, Mecca had seemed a sapphire city, an emerald city, a city of light so precious it could illuminate the darkest recesses of the heart of man.

He had been enchanted by the eternal light of Mecca and knew most certainly that this city was the closest man could come to paradise. Heaven was like Mecca. From that day forward, for Faisal, heaven had seemed real and attainable if he were but righteous enough.

And now he had come here for the second time in his middle years, by jet, for a pilgrimage of sacrifice and sorrow. He had come for strength and solace. He had come not in joy but in grief to pray for guidance to mend his shattered life.

In preparation for his moment on this mountain, Faisal had flown yesterday from Dhahran to Jeddah and then taken the pilgrim bus forty-five miles north. As he had entered Mecca by the serene and heavenly Gate of Peace, he had sighed as he sighed at his first glimpse of the black cube of the Kaaba majestically towering fifty feet high in the courtyard. He and all the world's eight hundred million Muslims prayed five times each day facing this sacred rock that was the 'Bet Allah,' the 'House of God.' For all time, at the beginning of time, at the creation, God had placed his Kaaba just here. Even in pagan times, men had worshipped at this shiny meteorite. But then this rock had been consecrated to the One God by the Prophet Abraham. Yet even after that, dark shadows had fallen again on this House of God, for after Abraham the idolatrous had set up their graven images again inside the Kaaba's sacred walls. It wasn't until the Prophet Muhammad was born thirteen centuries ago not far from the shade cast by this sacred stone that the Kaaba was once again consecrated purely to Allah.

Faisal had paced alone then through the opening rituals of the 'hajj,' for other pilgrims had begun their prayers here days ago. As he walked counterclockwise round the Kaaba seven times, chanting his prayers, he had hoped for a flood of understanding, acceptance, and peace. But he had remained troubled even as he proceeded to the next rites of the 'hajj.' He had drunk thirstily from the rich mineral water of the Sacred Well of Zamzam, symbol of Allah's font of mercy for the believers, and yet his soul had still been parched, He had run the course of the pious, seven times between the hills of Safu and Marwah, and then he had prayed inside the Sacred Mosque.

Finally, last night in the village of Mina he had camped humbly in the open on the rocky ground beside more than a million of the pious. He lay that night under the diamond stars that lit the sky above the holy city.

And now Faisal stood among the multitudes praying on the crest of Jebel el-Rahmah. It was a small mountain as mountains go, only two hundred feet high, a shortfall of mercy just outside Mecca. Beside Faisal prayed thousands of other Muslims. Spread below them, all around them, on the wide dusty Plain of Abraham, more than one million stood and prayed in the sun, where the Prophet had once stood and prayed in the sun. 'Wuquf' – 'the standing' – is the most sacred stie of the 'hajj,' the heart of the ritual. Since noon the weary pilgrims had been standing so and praying so, and it was now just before sunset.

Faisal prayed that Allah would give him the grace to know His will and then the strength to submit. 'Inshallah' – if God will it – he would forget about the infidel Nicole and devote all his attention to the cousin promised him in marriage - but he still felt in his bones that without Nicole his life from now on would be as barren and joyless as these desolate mountains in which holy Mecca nestled like a precious jewel. On the crest of the Mount of Mercy, Faisal prayed not for mercy but for strength.

"Doubly at Thy service, O God," he said in Arabic to the God he was sure was listening. Again, he repeated the 'Talbiyah,' the prayer of dedication and submission to the will of Allah which is uttered again and again by every pilgrim seeking God's sacred way. "Doubly at Thy service, O God."

In the distance a cannon boomed and the time for the 'standing' was over. The pilgrims surged to a rocky place called Muzdalifah. Faisal walked with the others, prayed with the others, and before he lay on the ground to try to sleep through the night, he bent with the others to gather his own forty-nine sharp pebbles to use in the rituals still to come. All that long night he lay sleepless in a fever of prayers for Allah to show him the way.

"Doubly at Thy service, O God."

Before daybreak another signal cannon boomed, and again the army of the faithful marched on Mina. A great and angry roar came from the throats of the Muslims when finally, they could see looming before them three square, whitewashed masonry pillars which symbolized Satan.

Once, very long ago, deep in the racial and religious memory, legend had it that on this very site the devil had tempted the Prophet Abraham to disobey God's command to sacrifice his son, whom the Muslims call not Isaac but Ishmael. But here, just here, Abraham had resisted Satan, and good had triumphed over evil. Faisal took one of his pebbles in his hand and threw it straight and true. A rain of pebbles beat against the pillars as the believers stoned the devil, repudiating all the evils of the world. Faisal took aim and threw another righteous rock. Nicole? Faisal cast again, until he had cast ten stones. Yet still he felt the evil with him, inside him, unpurged.

"Doubly at Thy service, O God," he prayed.

With the other pilgrims Faisal began the 'Eid el-Adha,' the Feast of Sacrifice. He bought a live young sheep from the herds brought to this place by the townsmen from neighboring villages and the Bedouin from the neighboring tribes. He murmured a prayer of consecration, and then with a sharp knife he slit the animal's throat. A river of sacrificial blood spurted on the dry Plain of Abraham. Faisal stared down at his slaughtered lamb, then at the blood dripping from his knife.

Long ago, here, the Prophet Abraham had been willing to sacrifice to God his Ishmael, his son who was the dearest thing on earth to him. After that testament of faith, long ago, here, God had taken pity on Abraham and accepted instead the sacrifice of a lamb. Today, here, the sacrifice of these animals symbolized he readiness of all Muslims to surrender whatever was dearest to them if that was God's will.

Faisal started at the blood on his knife. He raised his eyes to the heavens. Was God commanding him to renounce not only the memory of Nicole but all the wickedness of the West? H wondered if there was some oblique divine purpose for all that had happened. If he purified himself, made himself like a sharp sure blade of Damascene steel, would he someday be able to strike a mortal blow for Allah against the infidels? As the blood dripped from his knife to his hand, still Faisal pondered guilt and retribution.

He gave the carcass of his slaughtered lamb to the religious authorities for distribution to the poor, then he trudged with heavy heart back inside the sacred gates of Mecca. He stood with his brother and sister pilgrims in the teeming main square. He joined the ecstatic throng circling the Kaaba seven times, praying all the while, meditating on the unity of God and man. He kissed the 'Hajar el-Aswad,' – the 'Black Stone' – embedded in the south-eastern corner of the Kaaba. "Doubly at Thy service, O God." Faisal repeated over and over until the prayer seemed to ring inside his head.

In a daze of religious fever, then, he joined the masses of the faithful joyously following the paths of Abraham and the steps of Muhammad. He, and they, ran back and forth seven times from one point in the square to another. Just as Hagar, the second wife of Abraham and mother of Ishmael, had once run desperately through the desert in search of life-giving water for her son. Here on the sacred soil of what would become the square of Mecca, the Angel Gabriel had appeared to Hagar, the angel had stamped his foot on the ground, and a well had miraculously spouted from the barren ground. Faisal, and the others, drank from the Well of Zamzam just outside the Sacred Mosque, in the square of the prophets and angels and miraculous revelation.

The 'hajj' rites were almost at an end, and Faisal despaired that God was not going to give him a sign. With the dragging step of a vanquished man, he walked back outside the gates of Mecca to another flat holy plain, where he walked devoutly seven times between two more eroded holy hills. For the third and final time Faisal walked back to Mina, where stood the three pillars of the devil. Slowly he took careful aim at the white pillars, and one by one he threw the remaining stones at these representations of evil, seven stones at each pillar, and more, until he stood empty handed and disarmed.

"Doubly at Thy service, O God," he prayed again.

He turned his face to Mecca; then he gazed again upon the Mount of Mercy. Yet nowhere could he see the slightest intimation of Allah's revelation of his will. He heaved a hopeless sigh and walked slowly back inside the Gate of Peace. He supposed he had been presumptuous to dream of private revelation. He did not need any sign from heaven, any bolt of lightning, any eclipse of the sun, any shooting star falling from the sky to the earth. He knew right from wrong. He knew God's implacable laws. He must forget Nicole and renounce the infidel Western ways.

Tears filled his eyes. Nicole! How he loved her! He loved her more at this moment of grief and renunciation than he had ever loved her when he held her in his arms and thought they would live forever together as man and wife. He loved her now with longing and with pain. He loved her, but he would have to forget her.

Faisal stared at the Black Stone embedded in the Kaaba. He bowed his head and let the tears fall on his white pilgrim robe.

"Doubly at Thy service, O God," he prayed.

Finally, wearily, he put himself on the hands of the barbers for a symbolic shearing of a lock of his hair, the outward sign that a 'hajj' was completed, and a Muslim consecrated to Allah. But Faisal though that the beginning of his bleak years, the years of his lonely crusade in the service of Allah, required a more dramatic gesture.

Faisal told the barber to shave his head bare to his skull.

"Doubly at Thy service, O God," he prayed one more time.

Chapter 19

Faisal had immersed himself with passion into the restructuring of the Middle East petroleum industry. He worked obsessively long hours at the Ministry of Petroleum. He was not the only Arab to sour on the West but was considered a radical in ultra conservative Saudi. All he wanted was a constitution for his country, a curbing of the unlimited feudal power of the royal family, and a more equitable sharing of the oil wealth. Yet Faisal had been intimidated into keeping even his cautious dreams of reform mostly to himself.

Abdullah Tariki, the fiery Saudi Arabian oil minister who had been most responsible for the formation of OPEC, had been fired by King Faisal when Tariki spoke up once too often. His replacement, Zaki Yamani, was as gradualist and pro-American as the King he served.

Faisal had married his nineteen-year-old cousin Aida soon after he completed his 'hajj.' Aida was eager to give Faisal a son, but she had already miscarried twice. Faisal arrived in London with Aida to see a specialist in Harley Street. They checked into a fourth-floor suite at the Dorchester Hotel, Park Lane.

He was also going to meet the broker in London who watched over his family's European investments before travelling on to Vienna for an OPEC meeting. His cousin Muhammad who also came with them would be acting as chaperon for Aida in London whilst he was away at his many business meetings. Muhammad would stand guard in the corridor whilst Aida was inside the suite.

Muhammad had observed that his cousin Faisal seemed to be in a terrible temper lately. He knew better than to inquire why. Since the royal family had nipped in the bud a military and civilian revolutionary conspiracy a couple of years ago, the pitch of paranoia in the kingdom had been so sharply elevated that it was no longer safe even to whisper words of complaint against government graft and corruption. To make matters even worse, the kingdom had also been in the grip of an economic slowdown, for oil revenues had not kept pace with massive Saudi payments to prop up the Egyptian and Jordanian regimes after the disastrous 1967 war.

Faisal stood at the bulletproof windows of the penthouse suite of Vienna's Intercontinental Hotel, waiting. He had waited, it seemed almost all his life. But on this October night in 1973, with his waiting almost at an end, he could hardly bear the tension of these final seconds, minutes, hours. Thoughtfully he stared at the dimming lights of the infidel city below him. It was late, later than Vienna or any of the West thought.

While this sparkling infidel city of waltzes and chocolate and 'Gemutlichkeit' slept blissfully below on feather beds, here in the penthouse of the Intercontinental long-overdue decisions that might soon seem a nightmare to the Viennese burghers were about to be made. Faisal watched more lights wink out, and he imagined all Vienna going dark before his very eyes. He looked out beyond the city where it was already black, beyond the Ringstrasse where the medieval city walls had once stood.

Twice in the past five centuries the Turks and their armies of Allah had swept all the way to the city's gates. Just out there, Islam had been turned back. Faisal did not think he and his would be turned back this time round. "Bismallah al-Rahman al-Rahim" – In the name of God the merciful and the compassionate – he prayed to Allah.

God had put that oil in the ground under Saudi and Kuwait and Iraq and Iran. "Allahu Akbar!" – God is most great. At last, the Muslims would use their oil as a weapon for a good cause, for the best cause. "Inshallah!" – if God willed it.

Faisal looked out at the dark Viennese sky, where an Islamic crescent moon lit the night. He studied the lie of the heavens and did not doubt that just as Allah had arranged the cycles of the moon and the constellations of the stars, he had predestined the precise timing of the chain of events that was approaching its inevitable cataclysmic climax.

A week ago the armies of the Egyptians and the Syrians had surged across Suez and up the heights of the Golan in a crusade of honour to win back the lost soil of Palestine. It had been a surprise attack on the Jewish religious holiday of Yom Kippur, the Day of Atonement. Faisal and the other Arab oilmen had already been en route to Vienna for price negotiations on Saturday when the bulletins about the war had flashed around the world. Already, even without this new outbreak of hostilities, the stage had been set for a long-overdue confrontation between the oil-producing countries and the oil companies. International market conditions had been pointing not only to a massive increase in the price of oil but to a crucial shift in the structure and the power of the industry itself.

But the euphoria of the stunning early Arab supremacy in the war had strengthened the resolve of the Arabs in Vienna. On Monday they had told the negotiator they wanted nearly to double the price of oil, from less than three dollars per barrel to more than five dollars a barrel. But the oil companies had countered with an offer of a seventy-cent per barrel price increase. On Tuesday, when the Arabs had refused to budge the negotiators had stalled and said they had to wait for instructions.

On Wednesday the Arabs had warned the oil companies that they had only until Friday midnight to accept their offer. Next week the Gulf oil-producing nations were meeting in Kuwait for a hastily called conference linking oil-production levels to the war. The OPEC negotiators said it was in the best interest of the oil companies to accept this reasonable final offer. 'Inshallah,' after Kuwait, OPEC might have a far more radical agenda.

Faisal looked at his watch. The oilmen would be trooping up to the penthouse at any moment. Time was running out for all the West, for the era of cheap and abundant oil was at an end. During the worldwide glut of oil in the 1960s, the price had hovered at less than two dollars per barrel. But in the past few years demand had finally outpaced supply, and in 1971 in Teheran OPEC had succeeded in negotiating its first price increase with the majors. Yet inflation in the West and devaluations of the dollar had chipped away at the producer-country profits. Even before the October war, the stage had been set for an entirely new pricing accord.

Faisal took a deep breath and reassured himself that there was no reason to be nervous. Even if the West refused the price hike, OPEC would unilaterally impose it. Faisal's thoughts wandered from the price wars to the real war. He and the other Arabs here for the OPEC talks had thrilled so to the winning news from the front. After the shameful humiliations of '48 and '56 and '67, the early victories in Sinai and on the Golan had tasted all the sweeter. But Faisal was worried about possible American intervention. What would happen if push came to shove, and the Americans had to choose between Israel and a cheap unlimited supply of Saudi oil? In the end would they choose love or money?

Now, even the ultra-conservative Saudi princes seem to be working themselves up into righteous anger with the oil companies for their exploitation of Mideastern oil resources and with the Americans for their unyielding support of Israel. In addition, the more reactionary forces within the kingdom were still wary of Western influences. The old religious leaders liked to say that the malignant infidel growths, from television and radio to airplanes and automobiles, should be cut out like a cancer.

Faisal and his colleagues in the Ministry of Petroleum did what they could to convert these Saudi angers and prejudices into what they considered rational and enlightened policies of economic self-interest. Faisal wanted Saudis to run Aramco and wanted Arabs to get a reasonable share of the astronomical profits. He wanted to slow down the rate of production and conserve Saudi's resources for future generations.

Faisal's specialty had become Saudi relations with other Arab oil-producing states, and he had spent increasing blocks of time at OPEC meetings and visiting the Mideast oil fields. He was one of the first generation of Western-educated Arabs who were ready, willing, and able to run their own industry. Faisal had long ago understood that Aramco and the 'Seven Sisters' oil giants had never paid the Arab governments more than a slight fraction of the profits from the petroleum industry. But what was different now in 1973 was that finally Faisal and his colleagues had the means to force a change. It had taken decades for the Mideast oil industry to learn the value of joint economic action, but finally OPEC spoke powerfully and persuasively for the oil-producing nations.

Faisal reach ed into the vest pocket of his dark herring bone jacket and pulled out a packet of cigarettes. His hand was trembling when he lit a Marlboro filter with his gold Dunhill lighter. He had accepted his first cigarette two years ago in a tense smoke-filled room when he joined the OPEC negotiating team. At first, he had felt so sinful he had not inhaled, for at home smoking was still officially frowned upon. But in time his yearning to be in the Arab fraternity had overcome his fundamentalist guilt.

The other Arabs chain-smoked as if the slim cylinder of Kent, and Players and Dunhill and Craven and Marlboro were written in the genetic code of their race. And so Faisal had smoked and watched and waited at conference tables and in luxury hotel suites with his brothers from Kuwait and Iraq and Libya. They had waited for the world's demand for oil to exceed its supply for the Arab states to be ready to act in concert, for the season to play the bittersweet trump card of Arab vengeance.

Faisal stood on the top floor of the Vienna Intercontinental looking down at the once proud imperial city sleeping below him. His time of waiting was at an end. Finally, even cautious Saudi Arabia was about to unsheathe the oil weapon and use its economic power to force the West to redress thirty years of wrongs against the Palestinian people.

Faisal and all the other Saudis lounging in this suite eavesdropped as Zaki Yamani bargained on the phone with one of the princes in Riyadh about whether Saudi would cut its production five per cent or twenty per cent per month. To Faisal there was a melodious music to any of these numbers, just so long as Saudi linked the delivery of oil to the West with international politics.

For years Faisal had despaired that King Faisal would ever dare to take this step. The king had been threatening for some time specifically that America must moderate its support of

Israel if it wanted a continuing supply of oil. Yet the Americans had persisted in believing Faisal was bluffing.

Faisal listened intently to Zaki Yamani. That familiar throb and thrill to the oil minister's voice meant he must be closing a deal. This time Arab unity was going to be more than coffeehouse talk. Next week in Kuwait, Saudi Arabia would vote to cut production back five per cent a month until America and the West pressured Israel to withdraw from the Arab territories it had occupied in 1967. Finally, Faisal would no longer be ashamed to call himself a Saudi Arab.

On the telephone Yamani was reassuring a prince that the oil companies had no choice but to accede to the price increase. Yesterday over coffee, Yamani said, one of the negotiators had winked and said they would simply pass on the increase to the consumers. More money for OPEC would also mean more money for the oil companies, which had never once turned down the possibility of an extra penny of profit.

Faisal heard Yamani's voice suddenly change and become velvety and deferential. The king must be on the line. Yamani said he understood that the king did not want him to leave Vienna without a pricing accord, that he did not want to throw the loaded issue of oil prices on to the floor of the Kuwait conference, that he wanted not to break but only to curb the West.

Yamani bid a hasty farewell to the king as a knock finally sounded n the door. Faisal lit another cigarette, sat beside Yamani and studied the bland closed faces of the man from Exxon and the man from Shell. For five minutes everyone had taken the orders for orange juice or Cokes or coffee, the Exxon representative talked turkey:

"More time," he said bluntly. "We're going to have to ask you fellas for two more weeks."

Faisal blew a smoke ring, and as he watched the blue haze hover between the Arabs and the Westerners, he wondered how these men could be so dense and obtuse. He studied the confident faces of the oilmen. Could it be that they did not understand that the oil companies were no longer calling the shots?

Zaki Yamani shook his head as the man from Exxon earnestly explained that OPEC's demand to double petroleum prices had caught them unaware. A price of that magnitude would have an impact on every fibre of the Western economy, and so the companies must take the time to go to their own governments first for approval.

Yamani was still shaking his head as he politely fulfilled his responsibilities as host. He handed one of the executives a glass of fresh-squeezed orange juice; then he prepared a Coke the way he knew the other one like it, with ice and a slice of lime. Solicitously, symbolically, mischievously, he squeezed the lime dry.

"Two weeks?" Yamani shrugged. "I can tell you, OPEC is not going to like this."

The oil executives continued to try to justify the two-week adjournment. They talked about national pricing boards and the mechanisms of democracy and the past thirty years of mostly smooth company relations with the governments of the Middle East. But the oilmen were talking to themselves. Yamani began consulting airline timetables to see how quickly he could whisk his delegation home.

The oilmen were not accustomed to being dismissed by Arabs and so they sat for a very long while waiting for Yamani to haggle back at them. By the time it dawned on them that tonight's negotiations were at an end, the Saudis were already packing. Finally, the two bewildered executives got to their feet and walked to the door. But at the threshold the man from Exxon paused until he finally caught Yamani's eyes.

"Zaki, what happens now?"

For the very first time, the anxious West was waiting for a cue from the Arabs.

For one long exquisite moment, no one in the penthouse moved, as the Arabs savoured the first luscious taste of victory. For one long arrogant moment, Faisal fancied that there on the top floor of Vienna's Intercontinental he was watching power and ascendency and world domination pass from West to East.

Yamani smiled a very slight dismissive smile and waved his hand airily at the oil executives:

"You'll be hearing it on the radio."

The oilmen shut the penthouse door softly, even respectfully, behind them.

Faisal was calm and silent and watchful as all around him in the Kuwait Sheraton, Arabs from Iraq and Libya and Egypt and Bahrain and Abu Dhabi and Qatar vowed eternal brotherhood and solidarity with those dying for the cause. In this second week of the October War, the tide had turned against the Arabs. The Israelis had launched a successful counter-offensive across Suez and had rewon the Golan from the Syrians. But here in this airconditioned hotel auditorium the OEC delegates still talked like winners. Some wanted dollars; some wanted blood; others wanted power, vengeance, and every last inch of occupied Palestine.

Even before this conference began Iran and the Arabian Gulf members of OPEC had announced that the posted price of crude oil would be five dollars and twelve cents per barrel.

But then at this meeting, matters had taken murkier political and economic turns. As soon as the radical Arabs insisted oil must be used as a political weapon against Israel and its friends, the Iranian delegation had hurried excitedly for Teheran. Iran would vote to raise oil prices but wanted no part in any economic campaign against Israel. The Shah had been selling oil to Israeli customers for many years.

The Arabs then launched into a daylong debate on how to calibrate their use of the oil weapon. Ever since the founding of Israel, Arabs had dreamed of using the economic clout of Mideastern oil against the Zionist state. In 1948 the world hardly noticed when Iraq stopped its pipeline shipments to Haifa. In 1956 Iraq and other anti-Western states imposed to limited embargo on Britain and France, but the United States filled the gap by sending its own domestic oil to Western Europe. Again in 1967 Arabs tried a short-lived boycott of the West, yet they had to abandon it when the oil companies again shipped surplus oil wherever the Arabs were withholding it.

Until the October War their strategies had failed both because international market conditions were against them and because the powerful Gulf oil producing nations were not united. But the Arabs vowed in the Kuwait Sheraton that 1973 was to be the year of the oil weapon.

An Iraqi was maintaining that they could not put a price tag on honour, on blood, on glory. He pleaded for the total nationalization of all American oil interest, the withdrawal of all Arab funds invested in the United States, the sundering of diplomatic relations between the Arabs and the Americans.

The delegates lit cigarettes, motioned to the coffee boys to bring them fresh brew and looked uneasily down at the figures they had been scrawling on the notepads before them. If they decreased production, would they be cutting oil production or their own throats?

A Libyan was standing on his chair as he shouted for the Arab expropriation of all foreign companies. For a moment the delegates were so caught up with his exciting rhetoric that they surged to their feet and cheered.

All the while Faisal and the other Saudis sat in a quiet huddle. King Faisal had made it infinitely clear that today they were to keep a steadfast vigil with the radical Arab states who were fighting the good fight against Israel. But they were not to get carried away and promise the Palestinians the moon and the stars and their homeland.

Even before Faisal and the others had met in Vienna Saudi Arabia had agreed to a joint economic and political strategy with the Egyptians. Cairo wanted to regain its Sinai territory, and Riyadh wanted more money for its oil and more recognition of its role as a world power. If in the course of this struggle, Israel was humbled and Jerusalem regained, all Arabs would offer prayers of heartful thanksgiving. But here in Kuwait, Saudi would offer prayers of heartfelt thanksgiving. Here in Kuwait, Saudi would vote cautiously for *modest* monthly cutbacks in oil production and *selected* embargoes against Israel's staunchest supporters. King Faisal still hoped his moderation would keep America from launching a massive arms airlift to Israel.

With hooded eyes and a sense of futility Faisal watched the others parlay the oil weapon. In the end all that would matter was whatever black words were said in the White House in Washington. Even as the Arab oil ministers were meeting in Kuwait, a delegation of Arab foreign ministers was cooling its heels in Washington as they sought a personal meeting with President Nixon.

Faisal hunched miserably inside his ceremonial white silk robes as the whirlpool of Arab rhetoric swirled around him. He hated sitting mute as the chance for his country's greatness slipped away. He wished with all his heart that the Saudi nation dared stand up and be counted among its brothers. He longed to shout that Saudi Arabia would not sell America one drop of oil until Israel was brought to heel. He did not care what President Nixon might say to the Saudi foreign minister. By now, he thought, even King Faisal should have had enough of this gossamer web of American lies.

Yet Faisal kept his thoughts and his fury to himself. He had been sent here by his king to hold the line against the wild men of the Arab world. And hold the line he would. After the Iraqis and the Libyans were utterly exhausted from pleading their militant message all day long, Faisal and the other Saudis smoothly stepped in and imposed moderation. Oil production was to be cut back ten percent now, and five per cent more every month until there was a Middle East settlement agreeable to the Arabs. In the meantime, each Arab oil-producing national was to be free to stop any and all shipments to any countries supporting Israel.

Faisal looked up at the night sky as he stood outside the Kuwait Sheraton waiting for the limousines to take the Saudi delegation to the airport. The bright stars that had seemed to light the Viennese night with the promise of so great a destiny seemed dimmer now. The great adventure begun so auspiciously last week seemed to have ended in anticlimax in Kuwait. Back in the desert the Bedouin said the heavens were dark like this when a storm was brewing. As the limousines pulled up to the curb, Faisal murmured an automatic prayer under his breath for rain. It was October, beginning the season of the life-giving winter thunderstorms.

He could not know that just three nights from now, the biggest storm since the triumph of Muhammad the Prophet was about to break over all Arabia.

Tensely, Faisal lit another cigarette: he inhaled three times in quick succession, then stubbed out the tasteless cigarette in an ashtray and lit another. He raised his hand to signal for coffee, and when the boy bustled over with a full brass beaker, he drank two thimble-sized cups. He pulled back the long sleeve of his white robe and saw that it was seven minutes to the nine-o'clock television news.

Faisal looked around the Ministry of Petroleum's 'majlis' conference room in Dhahran, at the pearly muted tones of the Persian carpet on the floor, at the massive mahogany desk Zaki Yamani used when he was in the Eastern Province, at the ornately framed portraits of King Faisal and his father King Abdul Aziz, and his brother, Crown Prince Khalid. Perched on each of the spindle-legged gilt French Provincial chairs ranged all around the perimeter of this vast room was a white-robed Saudi bureaucrat. Each of them had rushed here after frantic calls from Riyadh summoned them to stand by for an emergency. The king had been meeting with Yamani and the royal Cabinet all evening at Riyassa Palace. In a few minutes their decision on how Saudi Arabi would respond to the thunderbolt of America's financial intervention in the war in Israel's behalf would be announced to the world.

Two dark dwarf-like Yemeni servants carried in a twenty-five-inch colour television set and placed it in the empty center of the 'majlis' floor. But the cord wouldn't reach to an outlet, and the servants had to scurry off to find an extension in time for the broadcast.

Faisal tried to temper his rising excitement. There probably wasn't going to be any earth-shaking news, just another mildly worded rebuke cautioning the Americans that Saudi might be forced to take drastic measures someday if the United States persisted in its support of Israel. Faisal doubted that even President Nixon's shocking duplicity this week had shaken King Faisal's confidence.

Two days ago, in a meeting with the foreign ministers of Saudi Arabia and the other Arab states, Nixon had promised a 'peaceful, just, and honourable settlement' in the Middle East. What Nixon had not told the Arab dignitaries was that a massive American airlift of military armaments was already underway to Israel. Nor did he warn the Arab dignitaries was that a massive American airlift of military armaments was already underway to Israel. Nor did he warn the Arabs that the very next day he would ask Congress for more than two billion dollars in emergency military aid for Israel. King Faisal had taken Nixon's actions as a deep personal insult, and so he had gathered the royal family together to plot revenge.

The servants finally found an extension cord, they switched on the television set, and Faisal and the other Saudi oil officials sat on the edge of their chairs. Faisal cautioned himself that what he was about to hear would be just another serving up of lukewarm threats and ancient resentments.

On the screen the announcer cleared his throat and grimly began to read from a brief prepared statement:

"The Kingdom of Saudi Arabia is immediately suspending all oil exports to the United States."

Faisal was so stunned he hardly heard the announcer repeating his bulletin.

Until now more than six hundred thousand barrels of Saudi oil had been shipped every day to the United States but now all shipments were to be stopped. The announcer issued a dramatic call to economic war:

"At the instruction of King Faisal," the announcer read, "a 'jihad,' a holy war, is being called. In this 'jihad' it is the duty of all Muslims to back the freedom fight."

Faisal and hundreds of thousands of Saudis listening to this electrifying news on radio and television were on their feet and cheering in the kingdom's offices and coffeehouses and black tents deep in the desert. "'El-Jihad!'" Faisal shouted along with his brothers. 'El-Jihad!'"

Chapter 20

Faisal's thoughts trailed back over the past fifteen months since the October War and the oil embargo. How naïve he and some of the others had been at the beginning, when they had all still believed Saudi Arabia was leading a crusade to build a grand new Islamic world that would cleanse mankind of corruption. Faisal had been outraged when, in March of 1974, King Faisal had ended the oil boycott before Israel returned even one inch of lost Palestine.

All the embargo had done was enrich the oil companies and the Arab governments who catered to them. Even before the price increase, the Saudi economy had been so underdeveloped it had been unable to spend the nine billion dollars it earned every year in oil revenues. So, in 1974, when Saudi found itself with thirty-four billion dollars to spend, hasty and extravagant and ill-considered development had sprouted form the Red Sea to the Gulf.

The princes of the House of Saud grew even fatter and greedier and more impossibly arrogant. Airplanes full of Western carpetbaggers and con-men and pimps of all persuasions darkened the skies over Dhahran and Riyadh and Jeddah as they flocked to pander to the baser instincts of the newly rich Arabs.

Billions of petrodollars ended up in the banks and on the stock markets of the industrialized Western states, but a complex and severe international depression had been triggered by the oil embargo. Stock market prices had collapsed, unemployment soared, economic production faltered, and inflation spiraled. The Arabs faced an economic dilemma. The value of the money they invested in the West was eroded by inflation, and so Arab oil was worth more in the ground than after it was pumped out and sold and converted into shaky Western currencies.

Yet the investments of the recycled petrodollars in America and Europe had intrinsically bound the Arabs to the continued health of the Western economies. If they didn't keep pumping oil at maximum production, their Western investments would be at risk.

Instead of a glorious victory for Islam, the oil embargo and price increase had merely made the West suffer mildly, pay extravagantly, and learn truly to hate the Arab people. Faisal didn't know whether he should be proud or ashamed of that day last spring in Riyadh when he had final poured out two repressed decades of angry recriminations to the king. Passionately he had said Saudi Arabia should nationalize its oil and enforce a real boycott to bring America and Israel to their knees. The inscrutable king had listened politely to his every word, but the very next day Shaykh Zaki Yamani informed him that he was to be banished to Vienna to serve as a permanent member of the OPEC Secretariat.

The welcome rumble of the tea cart coming down the hallway could just be heard over the drone of the Iraqi minister, who was making an interminably elegant point about the price-cutting of certain grades of Gulf light crude. Faisal fidgeted in his seat near the miniature green-and-gold Saudi Arabian flag arrayed with the other national emblems on the green baize-covered conference table.

It was nearly noon on this Sunday morning, and the concentration of the seventy OPEC officials and their aides packed into the narrow conference room wavered. They had opened their twice-yearly conference yesterday with an agenda of routine business guaranteed not to make world headlines. Jet lagged delegates from the far-flung oil rich countries of the world, from Indonesia and Nigeria and Venezuela as well as the Arab Middle East, diplomatically hid their yawns. Any minute now they would recess, drink tea together for a few social moments, then disperse through the city to rest up for this evening's official reception at the Hilton.

Faintly Faisal could hear church bells ringing from across Vienna's gabled medieval roof tops. He felt a pang of homesickness and wished instead for flat roofs and a deep masculine voice calling the faithful to prayer, He was weary of his assignment to the OPEC Secretariat and sorry he was still banished to this cold place. Outside, under the slate sky, a soft wet snow fell on this late December morning. Below on the icy pavements alongside the Ringstrasse, Viennese burghers bustled about preparing for this week's Christmas Holiday. Across the street in the 'Christkindmarkt,' loudspeakers blared the gentle lyrics of carols.

Faisal glanced around the crowded room, alert to any slight modulation of tone among the always touchy delegates. Next to him Saudi's Zaki Yamani fingered a gold Mark Cross pen. Across the table Jamshid Amouzegar, the Iranian representative, stared with hooded cobra eyes at the Iraqi who was still delivering his flowery, predictable, speech.

Suddenly, from the other side of the closed conference door there were loud staccato noises, a rattle of broken crockery on the tea cart, then shouts and the sound of running feet. A current of fear coursed through the OPEC ministers. Bursts of automatic gunfire came from the corridor, the reception rooms, the library. The distinguished and their secretaries and translators dived for their lives under the cover of the conference table. In the hallway high-pitched screams were drowned out by swells of gunfire.

The lights went out in the corridor. From a rasping throat came a savage battle cry. The conference door flew open, and two swarthy men wearing shaggy brown fur hats hurtled inside brandishing submachine guns. As the OPEC ministers flattened themselves under the table, the intruders sprayed random shots at the walls and the ceiling. The women secretaries were shrieking, there was a terrified babble of Spanish and an African dialect and guttural Arabic, the floor was a tangle of arms and legs and papers.

"Yousef! Get on with it! Put the explosives there!" The command came in Arabic. "Down there! Down there!"

Outside in the corridor the battle still raged. A woman gunned down an Austrian policeman who had already surrendered, then killed an Iraqi security guard who tried to wrest her submachine gun away. In a flanking office another armed intruder grappled with a Libyan delegate, then shot the delegate dead, and finally pumped five more shots into the Libyan at close range before leaving his body to slide into a pool of blood.

An Austrian woman screamed and screamed as a man with wild eyes dragged her by the hair through the doorway of the conference room. Another gunman shot a telephone out of the woman's hand, then raked the switchboard with automatic fire.

OPEC delegates were herded from the hallways and the offices into the conference room.

"Down," they were ordered. "Get down!"

The smell of blood and fear lay as acrid as cordite smoke over the conference room. Four minutes after the attack had begun, three men lay dead, and six gunmen had captured the seventy most important oil princes in the world.

"Yamani! Where's Yamani?" One of the gunmen screamed in English at the others. "Have you found Yamani?"

"Allah," groaned Shaykh Yamani. Faisal saw the lips of the Saudi oil minister move in silent prayer.

"No moving!" The gunmen shouted the command in English, German, Spanish, and Arabic.

From where he lay under the conference table Faisal heard more shots, running feet, a moaning from not far away. Outside on the street there was a screech of brakes. Gunmen fired out the window, and from the hallway came withering bursts of automatic fire, screams, the terrifying thud of a grenade exploding inside narrow walls. Choking fumes began to waft into the conference room, and clouds of plaster fell from the walls and ceilings. Another gunman staggered through the door, sank into an empty chair and pulled up his shirt to show his comrades a bullet hole just below his navel. Outside in the corridors finally there was silence.

Faisal lay still while the enormity of what was happening seeped through him. Terrorists were raiding the OPEC foreign minister's meeting. The cartel of men who had been able to hold the world for ransom were themselves being held at gunpoint.

Dully Faisal wondered which righteous cause this particular desperate band espoused. In 1975, this year of international terrorism, every faction in the world was armed and on the march. Were these German or Irish or Kurdish or Armenian or Basque or Palestinian or South American? They could be from anywhere or everywhere, for the word hated OPEC for more than quadrupling the price of oil. They could even be solid citizens from America or Britain or France who were sick of being victimized by those they publicly called the thugs of the world.

Cautiously Faisal angled his body into a crouch and peered up at two slender dark-haired men wiring sticks s of gelignite to the windowsill. As they worked, one gave the other terse commands in the flat accents of Palestinian Arabic. Faisal shut his eyes and shook his head. He had hoped and prayed in these last moments that his captors were anything but fellow Arabs. Back in Saudi, Faisal had argued at the time was overripe for the rich and conservative Arab states to concern themselves with the needs of the poor rather than the whims of the wealthy. But the cynical, cautious royals had instead continued propping up the moderate Arab states and hoping and praying that the less-moderate ones would self-destruct. Faisal sighed.

Even if the Saudis had refused to make policy changes that might have averted this day of reckoning, still they might have thwarted the raid by simply tightening their meager security measures. But the Saudis had joked the OPEC was headquartered in safe, jolly Vienna, not in lunatic Beirut. In whispered asides, the oil ministers had reminded him of the millions they paid the PLO to let them alone. Faisal had been wasting his breath he warned them that the more radical fringes of the Palestinian resistance could not be bought off so easily.

Faisal's suspicious mind turned to treachery. Could disaffected delegates from Algeria or Libya or Iraq have provided the terrorists with floor plans and meeting times and even a secret way into the meeting room? Faisal lay prone, his face to the nape of the rug, and gloomily remembered that today's bloody work was perhaps not history's first Arab fratricide. He considered the bitter possibility that Arab brotherhood was nothing but a beautiful myth, more fantastical than the most fanciful tale woven by Scheherazade.

There were more hoarsely shouted commands. "Up, one at a time, up. Stand up!" Slowly Faisal and the others got to their feet, and they held their arms in the air in surrender as the terrorists frisked them. The oil ministers stared from the precisely aimed barrels of the submachine guns to the face of the terrorist who apparently was calling the shots.

The tall, steely chief of the commando squad searched the faces of his captives until he bared his teeth in a wolfish smile at Yamani and then the Iranian Amouzegar.

"You die first," he promised in heavily accented English. With the butt of his gun, he began to separate his hostages into groups of conservative Gulf Arabs, Third World ministers, and representatives of the more radical Mideast states.

As Faisal joined the huddle of frightened Iranians and Gulf Arabs, he feared the terrorists might assassinate them all in the next few moments. Faisal's mind groped toward a comforting verse from the Qur'an.

"To the righteous soul will be said: O thou soul, in complete rest and satisfaction! Come back to the Lord well content thyself and well pleasing unto Him! Enter thou, then, among the devotees! Yea, enter thou my heaven."

But instead of signaling his commandos to open fire the leader stood before them like a general about to scold his rawest recruits:

"Reactionaries! You are the prisoners of the Arm of the Arab Revolution!"

With his cold dark boastful Spanish eyes, the young chieftain took the measure of his cowering middle-aged captives.

"Some of you will have heard of me already, eh? I am the famous Carlos, the one they call 'The Jackal!'"

Faisal stared back in horrified fascination at the Venezuelan born terrorist who styled himself a revolutionary Marxist liberator of the world. Carlos had gunned down a Zionist financier on the streets of London. Carlos had killed two French gendarmes and a Lebanese informer who tried to question him in his Paris hideout. Carlos had organized an attack on the French embassy in the Hague and was suspected of masterminding the Black September massacre of Israeli athletes at the Munich Olympics.

Carlos was a seasoned killer, one of the darlings of international terrorism. Faisal's eyes flickered to the other members of the gang. The lone woman stood with her menacing machine gun at the ready; she looked more savage than any of the men. Faisal had already overheard her bragging to her comrades that she was the one who had gunned down the two guards in the initial assault. The wounded terrorist who still sat rubbing his belly was tall, sturdy, fair and surely German. He and the woman might be from the Baader-Meinhof gang. The three lean, hard-faced Arabs were probably younger than their lined and bitter faces made them appear.

Faisal bowed his head and silently grieved for the broken lives of a generation of Arabs like these two before him, young men irreparably scarred by the corroding impact of acid rage. Just a moment ago Faisal had despaired of elusive Arab brotherhood. Yet he cherished at least the idea of that Holy Grail. Still, he liked to think that Yamani's and his own chances for survival would have been better if one of these Arabs had been the leader of the raid.

Meanwhile the chilling Carlos paced back and forth before his captive audience and began to harangue them:

"Criminals! You have so much money, but do you help your people? No, you make allies with the imperialist enemy, the

Americans! You have the power to bring the capitalist world to its knees, and instead you join with them against your own people! The oil belongs to the poor people of the Third World, and to the Arabs, your brothers, the homeless brothers and sisters of the Palestine you have forgotten!"

Carlos pulled a seven-page typed manifesto from his pocket and began reading it out loud. Faisal heard Carlos denounce the Zionists, the Americans, and the Iranians and praise the Syrians and the Iraqis as he waved his machine gun in the air.

"Pay! We will make all of you pay!"

Carlos chose a British woman to carry his political manifesto out to the Austrians.

"Unless they broadcast our demands over the radio by three-thirty this afternoon, I will execute a member of the United Arab Emirates delegation. An hour later a Saudi will die. Then an Iranian."

Carlos took another page of demands from his pocket.

"By seven tomorrow morning, a bus with curtained windows will take us all to the airport. There we will board a fully tanked DC-9 with a crew of three. But in the meantime, they must send an ambulance for our wounded comrade, who will be treated, then taken aboard our plane in the morning. Every delay, every provocation, every attempt to hinder us, under whatever pretext, will only risk the lives of our hostages. Understand?"

The English girl nodded timidly as he handed her the manifesto.

"Then go!" Carlos roared.

As the door closed behind the fleeing woman, a tense silence fell. Below them on the wide boulevard of the Ringstrasse there were the sounds of trucks and police wagons surrounding the building. Across the street where Sigmund Freud once had lectured at the University of Vienna, sharpshooters trained their sights on the second floor of the OPEC building. Sirens wailed, ambulance doors opened, bullhorns filled the air with nervous static. At a command from Carlos, the Arabs shot long bursts of warning fire out of the windows at the police van pulled up in the snowbanks. The curtains were drawn then, the lights were turned out, and there was a dark collective sigh from inside the OPEC conference room as the siege began.

Carlos called for a transistor radio and fiddled with the dial until he found a station playing schmaltzy Viennese waltzes. He glided toward the window to inspect the explosives that his comrades had already wired from there to the centre of the conference table. He turned theatrically to his captives and then struck a match. As he waved it dangerously close to the dynamite, he watched the play of fear on the mesmerized faces. Carlos laughed, pulled a Havana cigar from the pocket of his brown leather jacket, and lit it. He drew on the cigar slowly, meditatively, and with obvious pleasure.

"Now," Carlos said: "Now we wait."

The muted pearl of the creeping Viennese dawn faintly stained the heavens. Faisal looked at God's light and remembered that in the desert Bedouin knew it was time for the dawn prayers when there was enough light for them to distinguish a white thread from a black.

It was time to pray, yet neither the captors nor captives so much as yawned or stretched. All through this long anxious night, the oil ministers and their aides had sat rigidly awake while the terrorists paced and glowered and showed increasing signs of strain. After all the gang took amphetamines to help them stay alert, the one they called Youssef had spent hours tossing a grenade from his left hand to his right, sometimes even loosening the pin with his teeth, before Carlos sharply ordered him to stop. The tension was so unbearable the hostages had sometimes even prayed of the quick deliverance of a police counter-attack.

The jittery night had been studded with comings and goings. The Iraqi 'charge d'affaires' had bustled in and out of his role as official mediator. The voluble, impetuous Venezuelan ambassador had arrived to pay a goodwill visit to his friend the oil minister. As the hours dragged, the Algerian oil minister had begun to assume an important role. He was seen talking earnestly with Carlos and the Iraqi mediator, the outside telephone lines rang repeatedly for him, and shortly after midnight he assured everyone there would be no more violence. In the dead of night, the Libyan ambassador had sidled inside for a mysterious private conference with Carlos.

And most of all, that long awful night, Carlos had seemed to revel in every moment of his role at centre stage. He tried out his pidgin Arabic on the oil ministers. He screamed on the telephone when the Austrians sent in trays of ham sandwiches, which his Muslim captives could not eat. He stalked the room conferring with his comrades, he engaged in rambling Spanish confidences with the Venezuelan oil minister, he played the solicitous 'caballero' with his handful of female hostages.

Carlos took his deepest delight, however in toying with the strained nerves of the Saudi oil minister. Three times that night he drew Shaykh Yamani aside and, in between threats to kill him, confided that from Vienna they would all make a madcap odyssey by air from Libya to Baghdad then perhaps even to Kuwait, before reaching their final destination in revolutionary Aden. There, at the foot of the Arabian Peninsula, after all possibilities for international publicity had been exhausted, the terrorists would finally do what they had meant to do all the time. Carlos waved his automatic pistol. The first round would be for Yamani, the next for Amouzegar.

Before dawn the stale air of the conference room was blue and thick from too much nervous chain-smoking. Ashtrays overflowed and crumpled cigarette packs littered the floor alongside discarded paper plates and cups. Faisal looked from the garbage strewn conference room to the paling sky and thought of dying. He sighed and remembered happier sunrises at home in a black tent in the desert.

He remembered a lifetime of Saudi's spectacular sunrises of mauve and bronze and gold. He yearned for the peace of the desert, its solitude, its certainties. If this dawn was to be his last, he would have liked a sunrise so glorious that it would assure him of the inevitable triumph of the forces of light against the darkness. But today the world was still draped in shadows. His eyes fell from the effete greyish European dawn.

From outside came the tremble of a heavy tread, the whoosh of air brakes, the crunch of wide tires forcing passage through icy snowbanks. One of the Arabs looked out of the window and gave Carlos the high sign. Like a film star Carlos moved through the forty European and clerical hostages he was releasing, signing an autograph for one, giving another a spent ammunition case as a souvenir. The lucky ones were led into an adjoining library, and the door was finally shut behind them. Carlos clapped his hands and told the forty-two remaining hostages to put on their coats and get ready to go.

Outside it was cold and dark as Faisal and the others stumbled up the steps of the bus. Carlos stood by the door; the webbing strap of his machine gun slung across his chest as he aimed the muzzle at his hostages. Inside the woman terrorist stalked the aisle, her finger on the firing pin. The Arabs carried an armory of grenades and ammunition and spare weapons. Carlos was the last to swing aboard.

Gently the bus driver shifted gears and the cavalcade began to wind its way through the deserted streets for the airport.

In the lead were two police cars, then an ambulance carrying the wounded German terrorist, next the busload of hostages, finally another bus loaded with steel-helmeted special-duty 'einsatzkommando' police. At the airport the scene was set for more guerilla theatre. Television crews had already aimed their lights, powered by portable generators, at the twin-engine Austria Airlines DC-9 that was to be the getaway plane. Cameramen, producers, sound men, and reporters crowded the tarmac in readiness for the live transmission of whatever happened. Hidden on the observation decks of the airport building, sharpshooters took aim in case hell broke loose.

Aboard the airplane, Faisal sank into his seat, rubbed his bloodshot eyes, and looked around at his fellow hostages as he carefully buckled his safety belt. After their nineteen hours of sleepless anxiety, they were all exhausted, rumpled, and bleary-eyed. The conservative Gulf Arabs sat in one silent uneasy nest. The more radical oil ministers from Libya and Algeria and Iraq formed another more confident and chattering group. The Third World representatives seemed alternately bewildered and frightened and as detached as if they were watching a television drama. The plane thundered down the runway, lifted, and was airborne heading south for the Arab North Africa.

Faisal leaned back and tried to discipline his overtired mind into rational patterns of thought. He brooded as he slowly lit a cigarette. If he died today, he would leave unfinished business. He had dedicated his life to using the oil to better the lives of his people, but perversely Arabia's explosion of wealth had destroyed the very way of life he loved. It grieved him to see so much Saudi graft and corruption and spiritual alienation. Especially he was repelled by the extravagant greed and decadent indulgences of the royal family.

The House of Saud had turned Arabia into a police state, with barbed wire and tank patrols and a network of paid informers spying on every level of society. But most of all, Faisal was sick at heart that the royal family had not used its bonanza of oil wealth to make Saudi Arabia an international moral force for peace and prosperity. Despite the magnificent lies and fanciful wishful thinking of the Saudi national propaganda machine, even in the kingdom itself there were still pockets of grinding poverty and not enough food for some hungry mouths. Faisal believed that the royal family, too, should have done far more to help brother Arab states where the poverty and the deprivations of daily life were an Islamic scandal.

Once, when he was a young man of fire, he had tacked a photograph of Egypt's Nasser upon the wall of his apartment in Texas. Once he and young men like him could have decided to be like Nasser and change the feudal government of Arabia into something truly progressive. Faisal hoped it might still not be too late for himself and for his people. It was not enough that he had once spoken his mind to King Faisal. He vowed he would be truer to his beliefs if he survived this siege. Yet he had been silent for so long about so much that counted, he wondered if he would still have the power to speak his own heart and mind.

The plane landed in Algiers where Carlos set the Third World oil ministers free but kept fifteen Arabs and Iranians hostage. After five frayed hours on the runway, the jet was airborne for Libya. The siege was in its second day, and the terrorists had kept themselves awake with the aid of drugs for thirty-six hours. The German woman crept into a corner of the cabin and began to cry – one by one the hostages fell into a fitful sleep. As the plane started its descent into Tripoli, the rains began, and jagged red-blue bolts of lightning lit the sunset sky.

"Home!" Carlos cried out in relief. "Finally! I promise, here the prime minister himself will welcome us! Libya will hail us as heroes of the revolution!"

But after being forced to circle the airfield for an hour and running dangerously low on fuel the control tower made them park on an isolated runway, remote from the airport buildings. There was a long spell of negotiations on the radio from the cockpit. Through an open cabin door Faisal could see a Libyan sentry standing guard on the tarmac with his bayonet fixed.

A sullen mist hugged the runway, and the rain still fell in torrents. Faisal was about to settle back in his seat to try to sleep when he heard muffled sounds of elation from the other side of the cockpit curtain. He crept close enough to be able to distinguish words. "Ransom," Carlos was saying. And then the familiar voice of the Algerian oil minister was assuring Carlos something about a 'Swiss account' and Saudi's King Khalid and the Shah of Iran.

Carlos mumbled a sum in the millions. The voices trailed off into exclamations and congratulations and laughter.

Soon afterwards Faisal and four other OPEC aides were released as a goodwill gesture, but Shaykh Yamani and the other oil ministers were flying back with the terrorists to Algiers. Carlos poked Yamani in the ribs, and taunted him, and pretended he was going to put a bullet into his brain.

Faisal emerged from the stale blue air of the cabin into the wet pre-dawn darkness of the Libyan airfield. He ran a few steps, he breathed in the pure heady air of freedom, and thanked God he was still alive.

He turned and looked back at the red-and-white Austrian Airlines jet sitting motionless in the heavy mist like ghost ship. He had thought he would die in that airplane, but instead Allah, in his eternal wisdom, had given him a reprieve.

Chapter 21

Faisal's wife Aida gave birth to a baby boy, their precious first child, in a private London Clinic after her successful course of treatment by a Harley Street specialist gynecologist. Shortly afterwards, Faisal was granted an audience by King Khalid who bestowed the title of 'Shaykh' on him. Though he was still expected to stay at the OPEC Secretariat in Vienna for a further year of two, the king had granted him permission to visit the kingdom as often as he wished.

Faisal thanked Allah for his good fortune since the end of the Vienna siege. He took a sharp breath as he remembered how he had trembled in mortal fear on the hijacked airplane.

Today he was driving in the general direction of the Dahana dunes for a morning hunt, having risen in the middle of the night to prepare. Yesterday's brief freak thunder shower had raised a live green fuzz of grass and fragrant wisps of tiny red, violet, and white flowers on the desert sand. What was good pasture for grazing wildlife should be good hunting for the Arabs.

                    William Agunwa

Faisal and members of his Al-Murrah tribe rode slowly in line, out into the desert.

They rode out into the wilderness not as in the old days, in a caravan of dancing black Arabian stallions and atop fleet white racing camels. This time, in the dawning of this new Islamic era, four generations of Al-Murrah rode out to their ancestral tribunal hunting grounds in a cavalcade of cars and trucks powered by the Arab oil that had made them the new righteous kings of Allah's earth.

Faisal rode in solitary splendour in the lead car. He was a 'shaykh' now, one of the leaders not only of his tribe but of all the tribes of Arabs. His white robe was silken, his black cloak was edged with gold, and his face was regal and imperious. He looked back over his shoulder at the cousins and the uncles and the nephews fanning out like an army on the march. They had come together to return to the desert and celebrate the change in his fortune and the fortune of his people.

Faisal rode standing erect, holding on to the handrails he had installed in the back seat of his custom-made Mercedes convertible. A cartridge belt crossed his chest, a hawk was on one wrist, a carbine was in his other hand. He rode in valour as his ancestors had long ago coursed over the desert celebrating their victorious battles. He cast his mind back to that first wonderful euphoria after King Faisal had proclaimed holy war against the infidels, and he had longed to sweep out to the desert. He had yearned to ride fast and high and far atop a camel up and down the dunes, with God's wind and sun and sand on his skin and his hair and his soul.

He had wanted to ride out into the desert at the head of his family, just as he was riding now. But in those wild dizzy days of the oil embargo, there had been no time for hawking and hunting and a manly gathering of the tribe. Since that October it had been one conference and negotiation and oil auction after another, as Faisal had plied back and forth across the Middle East meeting with other OPEC oilmen.

King Faisal's call to 'jihad' had been fervently embraced by the Arab world, so that one month after the embargo was imposed Middle Eastern oil imports were down to two-thirds of their normal levels. Western Europe and Japan had been heavily dependent on Arab oil, and so as winter approached brokers had bid in panic for the little petroleum available. An auction of oil in Iran in December had brought offers of twelve to seventeen dollars per barrel, and when OPEC met in Tehran just before the end of the year the oil ministers had boosted the posted price to nearly twelve dollars per barrel. Ten weeks after OPEC had met with the oil companies in Vienna, petroleum prices had quadrupled.

Faisal had savoured the sweetness of Saudi's international triumph. The West had most definitely been humbled. At the height of the October War, President Nixon had made a Saudi diplomat wait for days before he deigned to meet with him at the White House. Yet just three weeks after the oil embargo, Secretary of State Henry Kissinger had flown to Riyadh to beg for oil. Two weeks after the embargo was imposed, the European Community had passed a resolution calling on Israel to withdraw to its pre-1967 borders.

The Japanese had sent their foreign minister to Riyadh for emergency talks, and the sly French had signed a separate pact with the Arabs. Most of the needy nations of Europe had come crawling to meet King Faisal's terms. With an awesome speed, the West had begun at least to pay lip service to 'the violated human rights' and 'the legitimate territorial claims' of the Palestinian people.

But for Faisal more had been won than money and the promise of belated justice for the Palestinians. For him, the victory in the blood feud with the West was fiercer and more primal. He believed the West deserved every bit of misery the Arabs were meting out to them. He believed that for too many vicious generations the West had humiliated and exploited the Arabs and every other culture in the world that wasn't white or European.

He looked out over the harsh, parched desert where his ancestors had lived in poverty and privation since the beginning of time. Let the West suffer.

Faisal felt the hot sun soak into his skin and the hot wind beat against his robes. Let the West shiver. Faisal felt the powerful throb of the Mercedes engine under his feet. Let the West pay. Faisal felt like a lord, not only of all he could see before him in the undulating folds of the desert, but of all the world.

Finally, Faisal had thought, it's *our* turn. After centuries as a stagnant backwater of the world, Arabia had become the centre of the earth. Finally, after centuries of ignorance and squalor and humiliation, Arabs were taking their rightful place as 'shaykhs' among the nations of the world. Finally, Arabs and Arabia had gloriously come of age. Finally, they had cast off the role of passive victims to become powerful predators.

Faisal squinted at the sky. He thought he could see something moving up there. He knitted his brows together, he crouched as though he had just spotted his prey from atop a camel, he called out and pointed to the black speck flying almost to the clouds. He shouted to his chauffer to go faster, onward, out to the desert. As the car lurched ahead, Faisal untied the lashing on his wrist. He plucked the hood off the falcon and raised his hand and let the bird fly. Up it soared, as fast and true as Sufis say their prayers ascend to Allah. Then the falcon veered in pursuit of the black eagle that had flown too near the waiting hunters.

The army of Arabs waved their guns in the air and cried out in delight as the chauffeurs stepped on the gas and raced behind Faisal. The eyes of the Al-Murrah were fixed on the sky where the coming battle would be fought. Yet the proud eagle wheeled and banked and fluttered its wings under the sun, as though a mere falcon were not worth fight or flight.

The falcon came at the eagle like a surface-to-air missile. The eagle turned and screeched and faltered as it tried to make its escape, but it was too late. The smaller bird hit the larger one, bird screams filled the air, the Arabs fired encouraging rounds of automatic gunfire at the clouds. Finally, the mortally wounded eagle lost altitude, screamed one last time and plummeted to earth.

Faisal's car sped to where the eagle had fallen. He called the falcon back to his wrist, hooded it, tied it down, and stared down at the bloody gore of feathers and skin and muscle that only a moment ago had been a mighty eagle. He remembered how he had always looked down at the fallen eagle and tried to rejoice that he had triumphed. Yet as Faisal stood over the fallen eagle it seemed to him that the bitter flavour of revenge was not exactly to his taste today. He had imagined revenge would taste sweeter, too, when the king had declared 'jihad' against the West.

He felt his gorge rise at the sight of the dead eagle. A vague contrite sorrow settled over his spirit. Only a moment ago he had been so certain this just retribution was the will of God. He wondered why, then, he felt so sad. He remembered his grandfather saying once when he was a boy that he should be altogether certain what he was asking for when he prayed or he might end up getting something for which he had not bargained. But then Faisal was engulfed in the triumphant throng of Al-Murrah who had left their cars to gloat over the fallen eagle.

Faisal threw back his head and let out the ancient war cry uttered by his ancestors centuries ago when they stormed out of Arabia to conquer most of the world for Islam. "Allahu Akbar!" – God is most great! He waved his carbine in the air in triumph.

"Allahu Akbar!" From the throats of the Al-Murrah came a mighty cry, so that it seemed every grain of the desert sands rang with an epiphany that reached all the way to the heavens. "Allahu Akbar!"

A shadow fell across the sand, and Faisal looked up at the sky. Already a waiting vulture careened overhead. Even vultures seemed to know that there would surely be slaughter this morning.

Faisal stuck his head out to squint at the faint trail of very fresh gazelle tracks he was following in the sand. He gasped and pointed at a herd of seven gazelles silhouetted at the crest of one of the first of the Dahanal dunes. Two bulls, four cows, and a calf had been drinking from a small rain pool that sparkled as if it were jewels. But even as Faisal sighted them, the gazelles froze in place, alert to the approach of the alien vehicle. He gave orders for the engine to be cut. It was rare, these days, to see a family of the small deer-like grey animals all together. For a moment he wondered if they were in a dream. In Arabian poetry, as on the tongues of Arabian lovers, the highest praise for a woman who pleases is to tell her that she is as shy and trembling and graceful as a gazelle. Faisal was willing to believe the gazelles ahead were a mirage.

Faisal hesitated then shrugged off his scruples. He supposed he was too sentimental. Those were real gazelles on the rise ahead, and gazelles did make tender meat. He blew the horn as a signal for the others to join them.

"Yalla! Let's go! Hit the horn! The others will want in on this."

They chased the gazelles up and down three more dunes. They were gaining on them by they were still not within firing distance.

"Straight ahead! 'Yalla!'"

The gazelles, Faisal thought, were so beautiful and so graceful as they ran for their lives. The gazelles were so wild and so free, the gazelles were so frantic and had so little of a sporting chance that Faisal quietly ordered his driver to ease his foot on the brake. If he went just a little slower, if the gazelles went just a little faster, they might reach the safety of the high dune country just in time.

Someone just behind Faisal pulled the firing pin of a fat grey gun: "Ratatatat! Rattatat! Ratatatatatatat!"

The bullets raked the flesh of two of the fleeing animals. First one cow fell, then a bull. The others had been running just far enough behind to miss the line of fire.

"Enough!" Faisal roared. "Let the others live! We have enough meat! Enough killing, in the name of Allah!"

Chapter 22

In the 'hajj' season of 1979, which fell that year in November, a record-breaking two million Muslims had come to Mecca to pray. The hostels and campgrounds and hotels had been crammed with pilgrims from every corner of the world, for this was the fifteenth century of the Muslim calendar – 1400 Hejira – a special anniversary year.

But in these troubled times, the peace of Allah clearly had not yet come to the world. In this season Ayatollah Khomeini's Iranian militants had seized American hostages in Iran, and the Muslim world was divided against itself on whether this act of wild defiance was the work of God or of the devil. Muslim public opinion united, however, in grief and anger when the atheist Soviets invaded Afghanistan and began to persecute God-fearing believers. In the long hot Ramadan that had preceded the 'hajj,' there had been public signs of religious reaction even in tightly controlled Saudi Arabia. Posters had been tacked up in the souks warning infidel foreigners not to dare to wear gold crosses around their necks or to let their shameless women walk in the streets of the kingdom with naked arms and legs and faces.

Yet still, before dawn on this Tuesday morning on the twentieth of November, a week after the formal 'Hajj' was over, the devout continued to swarm past the tamarisk trees on the Mecca Road. The lame hobbled on their walking sticks, the sick were being carried on their stretchers, even the dead were carried in their simple wooden caskets to Mecca for a final blessing.

Salim ibn Abdullah ibn Bakr Al-Shammaa carried one such wooden casket draped in white gauzy shrouds.

He and the five other young mourners seemed to stagger under the weight, as if the body in this bier were the remains of a fat Jeddah merchant, or maybe an obese distant cousin of the royal family, or perhaps merely one of the porcine takers of bribes who haunted the cavernous walls of all the government ministries. But occasionally one of the pallbearers would lean slightly while he mopped the sweat off his brow, and inside the casket there would be not the thud of flesh, but a rattle of heavy iron and steel. This casket, and fourteen others like it on this road, carried Russian AK-47 rifles, submachine guns, and enough ammunition to stand off the armies of iniquity almost forever.

The heavy casket dug into Salim's shoulder as he and his comrades marched toward their destiny at the Grand Mosque. Faint stars still shone in the western sky, while in the east the horizon burned with the coming of the sun. It was cold in the predawn darkness and Salim and the others were covered only by the thin coarse cotton of their austere shin-length white robes. But Salim and his bushy-bearded comrades did not complain on their long, forced march toward the most sacred shrine on earth. Theirs was a holy mission, theirs was a march of consecration, they believed a higher morality allowed them to violate the taboos of their faith and carry their forbidden warlike cargo into the sacred peaceful boundaries of Mecca.

As Salim trudged along with his silent comrades, it seemed to him that every event in the twenty-five years of his life had inevitably led him to the culminating glory of what has to happen in a few revolutionary moments when they passed through one of the sacred gates into the holy courtyard of the House of God. Here, this morning, just as soon as a 'shaykh' intoned the dawn prayers, he and his fellows would strike a righteous blow for the purity of Islam.

They would proclaim the coming of the new 'Mahdi' who would return the brotherhood of Muslims to their lost graces and holy destiny. Salim was also determined to avenge the death of his father Abdullah, allegedly implicated in a plot against the House of Saud, who had been executed quietly in the dark shadows of a prison yard by one of the monstrous family of towering Nubians who had served as slaves to the cruelest letter of the law. The father and the grandfather and the great-grandfather of this foreboding Nubian had been the royal executioners, famed throughout central Arabia for the neatness of their bloody work.

The casket was so heavy it was digging a ridge into the muscle of Salim's shoulder. He reveled in the pain as a personal sacrifice. Today in the courtyard of the Grand Mosque at Mecca, Salim and his three hundred consecrated comrades would fire the first shots to proclaim the beginning of their righteous movement, foretold by the Prophet Muhammad himself long ago, to cleanse all Islam.

Yet the burden of knowledge of what was to come this morning weighed heavier on Salim than the weapons in the casket. Mecca was sacred ground. No man was allowed into Mecca even carrying a gun, much less with the intention of shooting to kill with it. What Salim was going to be part of today would defile the shrine. If they failed, and the House of Saud brought them to trial, they would face the death penalty for the capital crime of desecrating Mecca. A foreboding passed through Salim like a shudder, and for a second the bier tilted so sharply on his shoulder that the guns almost clattered out, exposed, to the ground.

Fear of detection and failure made Salim stand straighter and more resolute. There was no room today, he sternly reminded himself, for doubts about the inevitably of their messianic destiny. Their visionary 'shaykh' mentor Yahya had dreamed strange and terrifying and wonderful dreams about what was to happen today.

The first dream had shown Yahya that the new 'Mahdi' – The Right-Guided One – foretold centuries ago by the Prophet Muhammad, was already among them. An obscure passage in one of the 'Hadiths' – Traditions of the Prophet – prophesied that in a forthcoming time of tumult a saviour would arise to restore God's kingdom on earth: "The princes will corrupt the earth," Muhammad was said to have said many long centuries before the Saudi royal family discovered a taste for gambling and women and wine, "so one of my people will be sent to bring back justice."

The 'Hadith' said the 'Mahdi' would be called Muhammad, son of Abdullah, and that he would be a blood descendant of the Prophet and would be revealed at the dawn of a new century. Yahya announced that Muhammad ibn Abdulla Al-Qahtani, whose mother was of the tribe of the Prophet, was Allah's new 'Mahdi.'

A second dream had shown Yahya exactly what to do with the revelations. Just as the 'Hadith' predicted, the new 'Mahdi' was to be proclaimed to the faithful before the Grand Mosque at Mecca. The people would rally to him, they would make of him a battle cry, and the House of Saud would fall. From the sanctity of the Grand Mosque the 'Mahdi' would proclaim a new holy war – 'jihad' – and millions of pious Muslims the world over would flock to answer the call to arms.

Yahya's third dread was apocalyptic. There would be violence and death in Mecca when the 'Mahdi' was proclaimed. Where the righteous battle was joined, the white marble would run in thick rivers of red blood. Unholy men would come to battle against them, but Allah would make the earth swallow up the armies of the defilers who dared resist the word and the flesh of the 'Mahdi.' Ten years, finally, after the epiphany and manifestation of the 'Mahdi,' the Antichrist would appear to wreak havoc; then finally Jesus Christ would descend again from paradise to destroy the Antichrist and restore the everlasting peace of Muhammad.

Today, here, now, this morning, Salim and the others were to play their roles in the great drama foretold by the Prophet Muhammad so long ago and by his follower Yahya only this year. First the shots and the blood, then the holy miracle, finally the great Islamic heavenly peace. As Salim trudged through the stone gate and into the courtyard of 'Beit Allah' – The House of God – he repeated that sequence to himself as if it were an incantation. Shots, blood, miracle, peace. First the darkness, then the light.

Fifty thousand of the faithful were already assembled in the emerald city for the dawn of prayers that would usher in a new Islamic century. But this blessed courtyard that could hold a quarter of a million worshippers was so vast it seemed to Salim at first sight as though there were no men and women here, only he and his comrades and their caskets of arms, and the great fierce black cube. He stared at the meteoric sheen of the Kaaba that seemed to glow from within even before the rising of the sun. He would have liked to set down his burden of death for a moment and pray privately before this holy citadel. He would have liked to meditate and maybe even think second thoughts before the action irrevocably began.

But it was too late for prayers or doubt. It was past four o'clock in the morning, almost dawn, and Salim's comrades were weaving their way toward the front of the mosque where a 'shaykh' was summoning one and all to prayer. Muslims were washing themselves and lining up and bending and kneeling in homage to God. Salim and his comrades prayed with the others. But as their lips moved in the familiar words, their eyes were shifting the length and breadth of the courtyard, watching for danger, preparing for the threats that would soon be brought against them.

"Allahu Akbar!" – God is Most Great!

As the final words echoed on the lips of the faithful, there was a commotion in the centre of the crowd, a tussle, the microphone was seized, the 'shaykh' was pushed aside, rifles were pulled out from under robes shots were fired into the air, the public address system squealed and then Yahya's hoarse, excited voice screeched loud and clear.

"The 'Mahdi!' Behold the Right-Guided-One!"

Salim and his comrades bent over the bier, ripped aside the burial shrouds, tore open the casket, and seized their submachine guns.

"The 'Mahdi!' The 'Mahdi' will bring justice to the earth! Recognize the 'Mahdi' who will cleanse the kingdom of its corruptions!"

Yahya waved Muhammad ibn Abdullah's arm to the heavens: "The 'Mahdi!' Behold the Right-Guided-One!"

Salim and his squad ran, as they had been trained to run, to block one of the thirty-nine double gateways to the courtyard.

"The 'Mahdi!' The 'Mahdi!'"

But pandemonium broke out among the thousands of terrified worshippers even as Yahya's proclamation echoed over the courtyard. Men and women screamed and ran for the exits as the clatters of automatic fire came from here, from there, from near the entrance to the Grand Mosque and at the doorway to the Kaaba. As the gunfire continued, Salim wondered why Yahya was commanding his followers to fire so very many warning shots. He had secured his own gate as ordered, and as he looked to the centre of the square it seemed Yahya and his crack guard were doing all they could to restore order. They fired repeated rounds into the air, but some of the shots ricocheted against walls and hit old men, young men, middle-aged women. Blood-stained bodies lay before the Grand Mosque. Red blood flowed in thick rivers on white marble. Salim shuddered as he remembered Yahya's prophecy.

"The 'Mahdi!' I proclaim the 'Mahdi!'"

In the centre of the courtyard Yahya was still waving Muhammad ibn Abdullah's arm in triumph. A knot of zealots surrounded the 'Mahdi' and raised their carbines to the sky. They shot triumphant round after round into the air:

"The 'Mahdi!'

Salim waved his machine gun in triumph as well. He did not grieve for the dead as he stepped past the pile of corpses and made his way to join the company of the elect. As he walked, he saw that his sandals smeared a slick trail of blood on the shiny marble.

The 'Mahdi!' Salim shouted. "The 'Mahdi!'" He cheered with his comrades, he fired his machine-gun to where Allah surely watched and smiled from the heavens, and then he climbed the winding steps of the tall slender minaret so he would be ready to defend their sacred killing ground when the army of the wicked princes came against them. Thus, it had been foretold fifteen Islamic centuries ago by the Prophet Muhammad and thus, 'Inshallah' – God willing – it would be.

The eight days of carnage now in the fierce fighting at Mecca became the scandal of the Muslim world. Sacrilege mounted upon sacrilege. Gun battles between the followers of Yahya and Saudi National Guardsmen had left hundreds dead in the courtyard before the Grand Mosque, and for the first few days of the siege the terrorist sniper fire from the minarets had been so easy it was not possible to even remove the corpses. The stench of rotting flesh, grilling in the intense midday sun, had profaned the House of Allah. In the first frantic hours after the siege had begun, Saudi officials were perplexed about whether they even dared fire against the rebels, for it was forbidden to bear arms in Mecca's holy environs. But the learned Muslim 'ulema' had given the Saudi army dispensation to shoot to kill. Saudi soldiers were told that if they died in this holy fight, their souls would instantly gain entrance to paradise. Intoxicated by that heady promise, soldiers loyal to the royal family walked unshielded into rains of zealot fire.

But the followers of Yahya also believed their cause so righteous that to die in defence of their cause would win them heaven. The rebels fought like cornered animals. When one died, his comrades shot his face off where he fell so the secret police would not identify his body and take vengeance on his family. The gamey stench of the dead and the acrid fumes of cordite lay like a pestilence over the slaughterhouse Mecca had become.

Yet still, despite the best efforts of the elite of the Saudi army, despite the best advice of seasoned American and French advisers, the followers of the 'Mahdi' had continued to hold the most sacred ground on earth. If the rebels had made their stand anywhere else, the firepower of the Saudi army would have crushed them to the size of grains of sand.

But the Saudis could not level the holy citadel of Mecca. They had to fight the zealots inch by bloody inch with light arms fire. Finally on Friday, the fourth day of the siege, the government forces won the high ground of the minarets and the upper storeys of the surrounding buildings. American-made tear-gas canisters were thrown to cover the advance of Saudi forces, column by column, around the courtyard.

Then it was the government's turn to rake the exposed flanks of the zealots from the minarets. Slowly, inexorably, Yahya's men were beaten back by the superior government troops. By the sixth day of siege Yahya had retreated underground with his surviving rebels. They barricaded themselves in the warren of cellar supply rooms and prayer alcoves that honeycombed under the courtyard. Saudi officials told the world media they would simply starve the terrorists to death.

But the world, especially the devout Muslim world, was not satisfied by that answer.

The first sketchy news of the attack had enraged the Muslim world. But their fury had to be based in a certain ignorance, for the Saudi royal family had immediately sealed off the kingdom from the rest of the world as soon as the attack occurred. Telephone lines were cut, and the government hunkered down for what its officials feared was a coup to overthrow the House of Saud. Yet garbled accounts of the assault inevitably leaked out, and the first hysterical assumption made in Muslim capitals was that the Americans and the Israelis had seized the heart of Islam. In Iran, the Ayatollah denounced the West and called on all Muslims to unite and triumph over the hated infidels.

Furious mobs laid siege to American consulates in Pakistan, where two Marines were killed when the embassy in the capital city of Islamabad was overrun and burned to the ground.

But then more details filtered out of Saudi. Russian AK-47 rifles had been found beside dead terrorist bodies, and the rumour had spread through the souks and bazaars of the Middle East that it was the Soviets who had attacked Mecca, that this was an attempt at a leftist coup by the South Yemenis or one of the Palestinian fringe groups or maybe even some fanatic cells of Maoists who had been training in remote desert camps. But gradually saner heads arrived at the truth. Russian rifles that had been used in the recent civil war in Yemen still glutted desert arms bazars just across the southern Saudi border. It would have been easy for the zealots to buy as many AK-47s as they needed. Saudi leaders thanked God their own Red Scare had been so short-lived.

The Saudi royal family despised the godless Soviets, were embarrassed by the insult of Israel's existence, and had nasty but short-lived family spats with the Americans. But it was only the always bad neighbor, Iran, who terrified the power brokers of Arabia. Rich, militant, grasping Iran at some time or other had laid claim to virtually all the oil-rich lands lapped by the Persian Gulf, and the Saudi – Iranian power rivalry was complicated by passionate religious loathing.

The ancient bitter schism between the Shias of Iran and the Sunnis of Saudi Arabia and most of the rest of the Muslim world festered as though the blood that had been spilled twelve centuries ago was still wet and unavenged.

Not long after the death of Muhammad, Islam had split into two antagonistic sects over the issue of whether Muslim leadership should be inherited or elected. Wars were fought between rival caliphs, and in the end the most prominent blood descendants of the Prophet Muhammad were murdered. But the blood feud did not stop with those first martyrs. Those who had fought the losing battle to keep the Prophet's relatives in power became known as the Shias, and in Saudi Arabia two hundred thousand of these Shias were clustered in segregated communities in the oil-rich Eastern Province. Always the insular Saudi Bedouin had treated this despised minority as second-class citizens.

Salim could not understand why their fight appeared to be ending sadly, wrongly like this. He was now badly wounded in his left shoulder. Yahya had promised them a better fate than the fetid air of this tomblike tunnel. How could it be, then, that the 'Mahdi' himself had fallen on the fourth morning of the battle?

Half the face of the 'right-guided-one' had been blown off by Saudi fire, and the 'Mahdi' had bled and died every bit as quickly as the others. Yahya had never dreamt a prophecy that the 'Mahdi' would die like that. Salim could hear footfalls behind him where his comrades were. It was Yahya himself. He came to tell them he had decided they should surrender together after first wrapping themselves in winding sheets. When they gave themselves up to the Saudis, they would already be clothed for the tomb. Silently Salim wrapped himself in the shroud.

At last, they were at the stairs leading to the courtyard. Yahya turned to face his bedraggled band: "The fight is not over! We will give them our bodies, but our minds and souls are Allah's alone! Up there in the sacred courtyard, make them fight to the end to take us! To our dying breaths, we will resist! Cameras! They will have the television cameras there! All over the kingdom, maybe all over the world, people will see us fighting, they will see our faces, and no matter what the House of Saud says, they will understand our cause us the cause of the righteous!"

"Amr Allah!" – At the Command of Allah! – the cry was taken up by the zealots. Their battle cries echoed one final time along the tunnels. "Amr Allah! Amr Allah!"

At long weary last, they climbed up to where their enemies waited. They reeled when they emerged into the starlight. Then they saw the soldiers wearing gas masks and bullet proof vests, television producers with clipboards and lights and cameras. The Saudis closed a tight ring around them. The Soldiers manacled their wrists behind them and put irons on their ankles. The Saudi soldiers spat on them, punched them, called them blasphemers and defilers of the House of God. They gagged the doomed zealots before they led them away to prison.

Chapter 23

Salim's only brother Rada stood in the front ranks of the crowd in the public square in Riyadh. He stood with his head held high and his face set in a grim mask. It was Friday, the ninth of January, just after the dawn prayers, and Rada stood waiting in the throng for the executions to begin.

Today in eight towns spread throughout the kingdom, the sixty-three condemned Mecca zealots would be beheaded. In Medina, in Dammam, in Buraydah, in Hail, in Abba, in Tabuk, in Mecca itself and here in Riyadh, the zealots would lose their heads. They had been accused and convicted of defiling the most sacred shrine in Islam with murder. In a few moments they would pay for their crime.

Rada prayed silently for Allah to aid him in the coming moments. He had to stand here in the cold Saudi dawn and watch his only brother cruelly put to death before his eyes. Honour required that he stand here. To do less, to cower at home and bemoan fate while his brother's blood was being spilled, would bring a deeper veil of shame upon his family and his tribe.

Rada stared straight ahead. Around him stood many hundreds of men who had assembled from far and wide for the spectacle of Allah's just and sure retribution. Six men would soon die here in the square. Rada bit his lips before they could tremble. He watched the two police cars inch through the press of the crowd to the centre of the square. The crowd pressed forward eagerly as the doors of the police car opened, then recoiled in horror as the executioner emerged – the dire personification of death itself.

Rada moistened his dry lips with the tip of his tongue. He stared at the man who was to kill his brother. The Nubian executioner was kin to the enforcer the Saudis had sent to execute his father in prison. He was more than six and half feet tall, and beefy, with skin as black and gleaming as the night sky when there was no moon. He was wearing a fresh, starched, spotless white robe, a ceremonial bandolier crossing his broad chest and a broad black sash at his waist. Atop that sash was the scabbard of his sword. Rada quickly looked away from the instrument of his only brother's death.

The rear door of the second police car opened, and two guards helped out the first of the condemned prisoners. Rada's eyes bore into the tall form of the victim in his austere white robe. A broad black blindfold was wound around the prisoner's eyes, and his hands were tied behind his back. He watched how the victim walked, how he held his shoulders back, how he held his head high. He was sure this was Salim. The victim stumbled and almost fell. Salim was led to the centre of the crowd, where a large square of cardboard had been laid out in the dust. The guards made Salim kneel.

A loudspeaker crackled with static; then a hoarse dire avenging voice sounded the length of the square: "There is no God but God, and Muhammad is the Messenger of God."

Rada stared grimly ahead as the deep voice told of the freely confessed crimes of Salim bin Abdullah bin Bakr Al-Shammaa. Rada recoiled when he heard his brother's name, but the carefully controlled muscles of his face did not betray him. He hated the House of Saud from Abdul Aziz, with his progeny of seventy-seven boys and fifty girls, to the present King Khalid, as the sing-song monotone over the loudspeaker rehearsed the well-known facts: how Salim and his comrades had seized the Grand Mosque, killed twenty-five hostages, killed one hundred and seventy-six government soldiers, and caused the deaths of at least seventy-five of the zealot criminals themselves.

The accusing voice droned on and on. Rada took a deep breath and willed himself not to think of anything at all. He must stand erect and unwavering and endure the horrors of these next few minutes. Others would be watching him, judging him, suspecting him, in these next moments. He swallowed hard. He would pretend this was only a television drama made by the Egyptians or the British or the Americans. He would delude himself that the evidence of his eyes was as lie. He would watch what must happen, but he would not really see it. His eyes would seem to watch the executioner, but he would focus to the right of where Salim knelt and waited.

Rada stared as if his life depended on it, as if his brother's life depended on it, at a guard who fidgeted in the sun. The guard was tall, young, and grim of face. He looked out at the crowd, waved, and motioned some message to his friends.

Rada concentrated on that guard. He tried to create an entire history for him. He was probably a fellow Shammaa tribesmen whose ancestral grazing lands were on the other side of Riyadh, a Shammaa whose grandfathers had raised camels and prayed for good grazing land and lived simple free uncomplicated lives by the grace of Allah.

Rada stood unmoving, watching that guard, as the voice of doom inexorably continued over the loudspeaker. An Islamic court had met privately to try the criminals for their crimes. They had been found guilty of murder and of desecrating Mecca. King Khalid himself had determined these men must die for their crimes.

"In the name of Allah, this prisoner must die!"

The crowds sighed as the voice stopped. The crowd craned their necks as the executioner neatly rolled up the right sleeve of his robe. The crowd surged forward as the executioner drew his sword from its scabbard in one long clean graceful sweeping movement. He brandished the sword above his head, pointing toward heaven. The sunlight caught the gleam of the shining double-edged Arabian blade. It was an old sword, a relic of past Bedouin campaigns in the desert. It was a long sword, three feet long and curving. It was a newly sharpened sword. The crowd caught its breath as the executioner nodded, as a guard deftly pricked Salim's skin with a sharp stick, and Salim's neck stiffened in a quick automatic reflex.

The executioner whirled the sword above his head as he took four prancing warm-up steps; and then he swung that sword as high as he could. With one great mighty merciful woosh he brought the blade down hard, fast, for one swift bloody instant of butchery. A fountain of scarlet blood spurted five to six feet into the air. Salim's trunk quivered, convulsed, twitched, then fell forward onto the sodden cardboard.

The crowd gasped, then roared its approval that Mecca murder had been punished. One guard picked up Salim's severed head and put it on a waiting stretcher. Two other guards lifted up Salim's body and placed it with the head on the stretcher. They loaded Salim's body into an ambulance.

The executioner cleaned the blood off his sword. A squad of Yemeni workmen remove the cardboard, wet and sticky with Salim's blood, then placed a fresh piece down in the dust of the square.

As the ambulance carrying Salim's body inched away through the crowd, another police car carrying the second condemned Mecca zealot moved slowly toward the centre of the square.

Rada turned, and as he began to make his way through the tightly packed press of onlookers, the crowd parted before him. Silently he walked through the crowd. He would have to go home and wash Salim's body and bury him before sundown, with his severed head turned to face Mecca even in his grave.

Rada's grim consolation came as he recalled how he had raised a glass or two in honour of the passing of dour old King Faisal. Because less than two years after he declared his 'jihad' against the West, Faisal had been shot by a nephew who resented being hauled back to Saudi after disgracing himself with drugs and women in America.

Rada's father Shaykh Abdullah Al-Shammaa had been vocal in condemning the graft, corruption, and excesses of the royal princes, and in the height of the paranoia after the royal family had nipped a military and civilian revolutionary conspiracy in the bud, Shaykh Abdullah was arrested for treason, imprisoned, and executed.

Rada again recalled with grim consolation that, like Salim, the nephew who had assassinated King Faisal also had his head cut off in the same main square in Riyadh.

Chapter 24

As soon as Peter, Paul, Frank, and I arrived at the Military Hospital we were conducted round the hospital departments by the American Medical Director, Dr. John Dean. We had coffee with him and a brief chat, were issued with our beepers and name badges, then driven to the residential compound about five kilometers away to rest up and unpack.

This compound had a high chain-link fence with an assortment of sanitized, air-conditioned, prefabricated bungalows, chalets, and villas with a look of Little America about it, complete with softball teams, garden clubs, bowling leagues, tennis clubs, swimming clubs, kindergartens, movie shows, and a commissariat supermarket for immediate shopping needs.

The compound had originally been built for and occupied by American experts on loan to the Saudi government for the planning and construction of the nearby highly sensitive multi-billion-dollar military base with its underground runways and silos. The majority of the American experts and their families had now left, and their accommodation was made available to the senior medical staff and administrators employed by the company running the military hospital on contract. The compound had been granted special privileges like less rigid separation of the sexes in social activities and less censored reading materials and movie shows. But regular patrols by the Saudi military intelligence officers and their Sudanese contract security men made sure no flagrant violation of Islamic customs went uncensored or unreported, followed usually by a written cautionary warning not to repeat the offending action on pain of instant deportation. Movement in and out of the compound was rigidly controlled by means of identity passes.

Three months after our arrival Peter Jacobs, Frank O'Neill, Paul van Waveren and I had established a routine of taking long walks on our day off on Fridays, the local equivalent of our Sunday, often to the bustling souk a few kilometers beyond the compound grounds. On these walks we are able to let off steam on subjects ranging from the hardships of life in Saudi to hospital and residential compound gossip, bizarre professional incidents, and the endless concern about what the exchange rates in the money markets were doing to our take-home riyals at the end of the month, as well as how best to invest for the maximum returns.

The Western women in the residential compound fumed about not being allowed to drive cars outside the confines of the compound and longed to escape what they regarded as a kennel which they could only leave if escorted by their husbands, as if they were dogs on very short leashes.

On one of our walks Peter told the story of Aliya. She had been rushed in late one night in a Toyota pick-up van as an obstetric emergency. Peter had to do an emergency caesarian section and as he said: "It was touch and go for a while… another hour or two and it would have been too late."

"What was the matter?" I inquired.

"Atresia. I've lately seen a lot of cases like Aliya. Sometimes we can save them, sometimes not. The only way we'll ever be able to lick this is by education. I suppose. Ignorance!" Peter's eyes blazed as though ignorance were anathema.

"It's like this," Peter went on with emotion. "Some of the women of Aliya's tribe – and apparently in the more primitive tribes around the Gulf as well – don't want their vaginas to be stretched out after they have had a baby. So just after childbirth a woman packs her birth canal with rock salt. From what we've been able to figure out, the women do this because they're afraid their husbands won't want them, that they'll be divorced and sent back to their fathers, unless their vaginas are as tight and snug as a virgin's for sexual intercourse. We're told that usually the women do this when they're having trouble with their marriages, when the husband is either threatening divorce or to take another younger or prettier wife. To hold on to their man, they pack their vaginas with rock salt so their husbands will like them better in bed. It must be agonizing when they put salt on their raw skin like that, but the real trouble doesn't begin until after they get pregnant. Some of them abort their fetuses. Others, like Aliya, get along fine until they are in labour. The fetus presses down, but the walls of the vagina are as solid as a rock. Unless we can get to the woman in time, and preform a caesarian, both the mother and the baby die. It's a terrible thing…"

We were astounded. Frank who had anaesthetized for Peter during the operation nodded his head sadly in agreement with Peter's sentiments. Peter continued: "What Aliya had done to herself was almost as bad as the routine genital mutilation of every little Saudi girl. Aunts cut off the clitoris of little girls with a pair of rusty scissors. This is done to the girls before puberty so that they would not be wild and act as bad as prostitutes."

Paul was concerned about the number of children he had seen in his clinic with cautery burns prescribed by Arabic doctors for every and any ailment where there is local pain, some of these burns turned septic. However, he was impressed by how children, especially boys, were treasured by the Saudis. Paul also remarked how the overwhelming outdoor activity and hobby of young Saudis seemed to be 'koorah' – football – and nothing much else. He was particularly worried that children as young as nine or ten years old could be found behind the wheels of cars and Land-Rovers on public roads.

We all agreed that driving on Saudi highways was unusually risky. For one thing, if you had a breakdown of any description especially in the remote areas, your fate was in the lap of the gods; you were most unlikely to get help from passing vehicles, and you couldn't telephone for help marooned in the vast stretches of the desert asphalt highways. On the berm of the road every few miles or so were rusty wrecked Buicks and Chevrolets and Toyotas and Datsuns and Land-Rovers left to decay where they had stopped, just as camel carcasses had once been left to rot to white bleached bones beside caravan trails.

The greatest hazard was perhaps the Saudi drivers; to them the machismo of overtaking you at all costs seemed to count for everything. And of course, if you were involved in any accident with a Saudi, even if he bumped into you whilst you are parked or stationary, you're *a priori* the guilty party.

The other great hazard of travelling on Saudi highways was undoubtedly camels crossing the road at blind corners and at night. The commonest cause of lethal neck injuries in these parts seemed to be vehicular confrontations with camels, the camel thumping your head and neck through the roof of the car.

Then as the summer months approach, driving on long distance Saudi roads simulates driving in soup fog conditions when swirling oceans of beige desert sand drifts over onto the narrowed asphalt ribbon of the highway. The suddenness of the sandstorms and vortices especially when driving at speed or trying to avoid those driving at greater speed compounds the danger. Windscreens are often irreparably frosted and damaged when ferociously bombarded by the accelerated atomic sand particles, when using your windscreen wiper at the height of the storm only makes things worse.

Chapter 25

Six months into my contract the flight ticket for my earned benefit leave arrived. I had decided to stop over in Athens on my way to London. Our departure was uneventful and the flight itself was pleasant with good food and a few empty seats to spread into. But a few minutes before we were to begin our descent to Athens we heard a scuffle in the cockpit and suddenly three gunmen proclaiming themselves to be resistance fighters from the Popular Front for the Liberation of Palestine stalked the aisle of the plane pulling shut the window shades, checking their grenades and ammunition and holding their guns in firing positions. The pilot was ordered to fly to Libya.

One terrorist stood in the cockpit with a gun melodramatically held to the pilot's head whilst the other two prowled the aisle.

I sank into my seat, rubbed my eyes to make sure I wasn't dreaming, and looked around at my fellow hostages as I carefully buckled my safety belt. I brooded as I felt alternatively bewildered and frightened and as detached as if I were watching a television drama. I tried to discipline my disordered mind into rational patterns of thought. If I died today, I would leave unfinished business. Outwardly Rachel and I were separated, but inwardly I have never stopped loving her. I had in fact been in touch with her by telephone three times since my arrival in Saudi Arabia, and I had spoken to her a couple of days ago to inform her about my flight plans. I vowed I would try to make a fresh start with Rachel. But did she still love me? I wanted to live to find out. Please God, I prayed, let me live.

As the nervous minutes ticked by on the hijacked plane, the terrorists began to toy with their grenades. One of the so-called Palestinians spoke in the rushed blurry accents of a Lebanese. The other one prowling the aisle seldom spoke, but by his round cherub face, his squat peasant body, and his bronzed brown skin he could as well have been from one of the Dhofar guerilla units fighting their sporadic Omani 'people's war' on the revolutionary southern fringe of the Arabian Peninsula.

We overheard the putative leader of the terrorists shouting into the cockpit radio that of course he had permission to land at Tripoli. But the plane levelled off and began circling the airfield. The other terrorists seemed more agitated now than in the first moments of the hijack. The Americans on the plane were huddled into one silent uneasy nest. One of the Americans, bearded, and with a Jewish sounding name was forced to lie on his face near the lavatory and was cold-bloodedly shot through the head. A couple of minutes later permission was granted for us to begin our descent to Tripoli.

After the plane shuddered to a stop, one of the terrorists stood guard with his gun aimed at the rear door. The terrorists played out a period of tense negotiations with their supposed Libyan friends. To my great and unexpected surprise, I was one of the six hostages set free at Tripoli as a gesture of goodwill.

I emerged from the stale air of the cabin into the shimmering head of the Libyan airfield. I ran a few steps and breathed in the pure heady air of freedom, and thanked God I was still alive. I dared not look back at the hijacked plane sitting motionless on the runway. I squared my shoulders and walked with the other released hostages back toward the airline terminal, and to a Libyan hotel room where after sleeping for several hours I finally awoke to the welcome news that the other hostages had been released in Algiers.

The following morning after I had showered and eaten, I raced back to the airport to catch the first flight to London, Heathrow.

I hoped against all reason that Rachel would somehow know I was on that flight and be waiting for me at the airport. I had been the one whose life was in danger during the long anxious hours of the hijack, but as soon as I was safe, I feared that somehow she had been struck down and forever taken from me. I looked down at my rumpled suit and ignored my appearance as I feverishly tried to rehearse a 'mea culpa' reconciliation confession, gripped by an overwhelming feeling that contact with her was now a life-and-death matter.

I took a deep breath as I approached the barrier and the crowd outside customs. I craned my neck to see if Rachel was there. Yes, she was! Rachel's face was swollen with the evidence of tears. The shine of recognition and relief in her eyes when she saw me stung my own eyes with hot tears which I failed to hold back despite trying so hard to keep a dry eye.

"Desmond!" Rachel threw herself into my arms. "Desmond. Oh my God, Desmond you're safe, you're all right, you're here. They said on the television one hostage was shot. I didn't know for sure who it was. Oh Desmond! I've missed you so!"

We held on to each other as we took a taxi to a hotel in central London. We rocked together in the doorway of our hotel room as if on the threshold of sanity after years in a madhouse of our own making. Our arms were intertwined as we shut the door behind us and sank down on the thick-pile carpet.

"I have so much to tell you, so much to explain," I began. But she put her finger to my lips. "Later,' she whispered. "We'll talk later."

I tried to kiss her, but she shook her head – 'Not yet,' and instead snuggled close to me as though I were a quilt, and she were cold and tired and finally snug in her own bed after too long a journey away from the home of my arms. My shoulder encircled her, her hand curled on my cheek, we sighed and were finally warm enough after the long spell of chill. When after a while my hand stroked the small of her back, she raised her head and smiled to let me know without words that our time of waiting was over.

Slowly we drew closer together; our lips touched; gently she turned in my arms so that our bodies pressed together on the soft carpet. There was a new element of tenderness in this kiss, a mutual desire not so much for the ecstasy of thrill and touch as for the comfort and reassurance of intimacy made flesh. I loved her with butterfly kisses on her cheeks, and her eyes; she loved me with the faint tracery of her finger trailing from my eyes to my lips to my neck to my chest. We kissed with a groping, growing passion until she staggered to her feet and led me to the double bed of feathers, and we undressed and lay under the eiderdown. For a long while we made slow gentle sacramental love with our eyes wide open. Finally, in the full faint sun of that London afternoon we fell asleep cradled in each other's arms.

About the Author

Dr. William Agunwa was born in Enugu, the former capital of Biafra, Eastern Nigeria.

In his early years he won an open scholarship to the prestigious Government College Umuahia and the University of Glasgow Medical School. There he qualified with a Class Prize in surgery leading to house jobs with the Regius Professors of Surgery and Medicine.

He continued training at the Royal National Orthopaedic Hospital (at both the Stanmore and London locations) and became a Senior Fellow with the Royal College of Surgeons and the Royal Society of Medicine.

From there he continued working as a consultant for teaching hospitals in England, Scotland, and the Middle East, including King Khalid Military City Hospital in Jeddah, King Abdulaziz Airforce Military Hospital in Dhahran, and Riyadh Military Teaching Hospital in Saudi Arabia. He also worked as the Chief of Surgery at King Fahad Specialist Hospital in Medina.
Besides working in the Middle East, Dr. Agunwa has also widely traveled across Europe including the Balkans, the Nordic countries, the Irish Republic, Ulster and has made several trips to the USA.

As an author, Dr. Agunwa started writing even before his medical undergraduate days with minor publications in college and parish magazines. During his career, he continued to write articles for the British Medical Journal and the Journal of Accident Surgery, going on to publish his first novel, Jobs for the Boys, in 1990.

www.ingramcontent.com/pod-product-compliance
Lightning Source LLC
Chambersburg PA
CBHW070350200726
48294CB00003B/827